THE BABY MISSION

JESSA JAMES

The Baby Mission: Copyright © 2020 by Jessa James

All Rights Reserved. No part of this book may be reproduced or transmitted in any form or by any means, electrical, digital or mechanical including but not limited to photocopying, recording, scanning or by any type of data storage and retrieval system without express, written permission from the author.

Published by Jessa James
James, Jessa
The Baby Mission

Cover design copyright 2020 by Jessa James, Author
Images/Photo Credit: Deposit Photos: gstockstudio

Publisher's Note:
This book was written for an adult audience. The book may contain explicit sexual content. Sexual activities included in this book are strictly fantasies intended for adults and any activities or risks taken by fictional characters within the story are neither endorsed nor encouraged by the author or publisher.

This book has been previously published.

GET A FREE BOOK!

Join my mailing list to be the first to know of new releases, free books, special prices and other author giveaways.

http://freehotcontemporary.com

JETT

"I'm telling you, women are all the same," I say. "They just want you to believe that some of them are different…"

Mason and Alex, my two best friends, don't even look at me as we climb the stairs leading to the roof. They've heard it all before, but they are listening anyway. They're good friends.

I huff a little as we hit the sixth flight of stairs. A small gaggle of women comes down the stairwell, their high heels making a sharp *clomp-clomp-clomp* sound on the concrete. I'm distracted for a second by the women, with their bright smiles and miles of long legs.

I like the look of the one in the front, leading the pack. She's a blonde in a pink minidress. She makes eye contact with me for a second, then blushes and bites her lip.

She's looking at me too, at me and Mason and Alex. Three tall, handsome men in plaid button downs and jeans. She's probably trying to figure out which of us is the hottest.

Alex is easily the tallest. At 6'6, he's got a few inches on me and Mason. It made the college football scouts come knocking when he was seventeen, too.

Mason has the whole dark and brooding thing going on, especially with that nose of his that's been broken a half dozen times. He draws women who are attracted to his angsty don't-fuck-with-me persona.

And me? I'm pretty fucking tall, I've got a good body, and I've got a great face. I unleash one of my dangerous smiles on the woman making eye contact with me. She stumbles a little, reaching out to grab the wall to balance herself.

Bingo, I think. It feels pretty damn gratifying.

And then they're out of sight. We come up to a plain metal door, and even though it's closed, I can hear the party happening on the other side. The wub-dub-dub of the bass can be heard through the door.

I push the door open, and step outside into the cool late spring night air. The party is on a rooftop, with lights strung overhead and a hundred plus people chatting and dancing below. Immediately, I'm engulfed in loud, poppy music and the big, bright colored lights that flash across the whole event.

"Jett, come on," Mason says, touching my arm and jerking his head towards a bar set up across the way from us.

I follow Mason, threading my way through the crowd. Here and there I get glances from women, which makes me feel perversely hopeful. I don't necessarily want their attention right now, but I might want it later. Once I get a few beers inside me, I may be able to forget about Emily and focus on what my body needs.

At the thought of Emily, I frown. Emily is exactly my type: blonde hair, honey-brown eyes, and she has a dancer's lithe frame. Emily is also the fucking bitch that ripped out my heart and stomped on it.

So there's that.

Mason spots an ice bucket filled to the brim with beer, and all three of us grab one. It's a Miller High Life, nothing fancy. I twist off the top and take a sip, feel the cool slide of the beer in my throat.

Alex leads the way to an unoccupied spot along the wall, and we stand and look out at the party.

"What's this party for, again?" Mason asks.

"It's thrown by my manager," Alex says with a shrug. "Something about the rites of spring."

"You guys are still hunting for another NFL team?" I ask Alex.

"Yep. I'm not quite ready to throw in the towel."

"You should be, after that nasty hit you took last year," Mason says. "I was watching the game when those three guys took you down."

Alex shifts, and it's clear from his body language that he doesn't want to talk about it. I used to be someone in baseball, so I get where he's coming from.

"Hey, did I tell you that the guys from my office have made up these fake draft card things? Here, let me get one out…" I say, pulling a card from my wallet. "They're supposed to look like baseball cards, but they're for the sports agents at Sampson ."

"That's not a bad picture of you," Mason says. Plucking the card from my fingers, he holds it up beside my head and squints. "You could really get some good pussy with this, you know."

"Not bad," Alex says, sipping his beer.

"Emily says it's a bad picture of me," I say, grabbing the card from him and putting it back in my wallet.

"Oh my god. Well if *Emily* says it, then it must be

true!" Mason says, rolling his eyes. "I am so sick of hearing her name. She dumped you for some stupid reasons, so let's just move on."

"It's not that easy," I protest, but even to me it sounds weak.

"It's been a month, man," Alex says, clapping me on the back. "She's probably fucking someone new. You should take your cue from her."

"Whatever," I say.

"Seriously, stop whining and get some action. Just look around this party. There are sexy women everywhere you look," Mason says.

I take minute to assess, and find that Mason isn't wrong. There are tons of girls at this party, dancing together or standing close to talk to one another.

"I think I see who I'm going to hit on," Alex says. "If you'll excuse me…"

He heads to the other side of the party, his sheer size forcing people to move out of his way as he shoulders his way through the crowd.

"See? It's that easy," Mason says.

"I can pick up any girl I want," I say, raising a brow. "I'm Jett James."

"I don't know about *any* girl."

"Seriously?" I ask, cocking a brow. "How about this? You pick the girl. And I'm willing to bet you Hawks floor seats."

Mason side-eyes me. "Alright, but you can't just go home with whomever I pick. You have to go on a date."

"A date? Really?" I say.

"It's too easy to just go home with a girl and never see her again. Come on, it'll be good for you."

"Fuck, all right," I say, rubbing the back of my neck. "Just promise that you'll pick someone good."

His brows rise. "I'm offended that you think I wouldn't."

I just grunt and sip my beer. Mason is busy looking around.

"What about her, the blonde in the red miniskirt? She's my type," I say.

Mason looks at me, slightly exasperated.

"You said that I got to pick. Besides, I am so bored of the blondes that you bring around. They are, as you say, all exactly the same. Short, skinny, and blonde." He makes a face. "You need someone a little different. Consider this your palate cleanser."

"Psshhh," I say, waving my hand at him. "You complain too much."

"Shh, let me look." His brows pull down in concentration. "Ah. How about there? The brunette with the red sweater and the skirt."

I look where he is looking, and after a second, I spot her. She's downright academic looking, in an attractive way. She has long hair, just the color of a raven's wing, and olive-toned skin. A pair of black-rimmed sunglasses rests on her head. She is wearing an oversized red sweater, a black pencil skirt, and a pair of cherry red high heels.

She's also holding a big black purse and fiddling with her iPhone. She made a sour face suddenly, and started typing something into her phone. The way her thumbs were flying, I could imagine that someone was in trouble.

She looks like she's smart, but she wouldn't be into the whole former-jock thing that I have going on. Which is just as well, because she looks like someone who is about to teach me English, not like someone who I'd go on a date with.

"She's pretty," I admit. "But she looks boring. Look, her friends are trying to get her to dance. I bet she'll say no."

A few seconds later, she politely rebuffed her friends' entreaties, and she was left alone once more.

"I have a good feeling about her," Mason says. "She's definitely the one."

"Come on, you have to pick someone more interesting," I say. "Like… anyone else at this party."

"I thought Jett James could pick up anyone?" he says, a shit-eating grin on his face.

"She looks like she just swallowed a whole lemon."

"And?" he said. "You said that you were betting court side Hawks tickets on it."

Fuck. "Alright, alright. I'm going."

I gave him the stink eye as I push my way through the crowd, heading over to the spot where she leans against the wall. I notice that she taps her foot along with the music, despite looking downright annoyed.

"Excuse me," I say, stopping in front of her.

She looks up at me, her gray eyes uncertain. "Yes?"

I like her voice, a throaty, velvet purr.

"I just came over here to say that you're stunning," I say. I wince a little, as the music suddenly got louder about halfway through my sentence. My words were lost.

She scrunches up her face, which is sort of comical. "What?"

I lean closer to her, and catch a faint whiff of her perfume. "I said, you're stunning."

Her expression turns disapproving in a heartbeat. There is a second where I can feel her eyes on me, feel her assessing my clothes and my height, feel her calculating something. She takes in the tattoos that are visible, too. And then I see dismissal in her expression, without knowing me at all.

She's essentially decided that I'm not worthwhile, based on some kind of metrics that I'm not privy to.

It doesn't feel good.

"Oh, uhh— thanks?" she says. I can tell that she's about to end the conversation.

Where's that famous Jett James charm? I wonder.

"Hey, would you do me a favor?" I say, without really thinking about it. "My ex Emily is here, and she's sort of slyly watching me. Is it cool if I just pretend that you and I are hitting it off?"

Her eyes have wandered down to her phone screen, but they snap back up to mine. She examines me for another second, her dark grey eyes like watching a gathering storm.

"Ummm..." she says, obviously torn between me and whatever is on her phone.

Damn, am I that uninteresting?

"Sure," she finally says, but it feels like I've only just got her to look at me. Time to be dazzling, I guess.

I grin at her, moving a little closer. "You'd tell me if this fake relationship was inconveniencing you, right?"

I see her worry her lip a little and furrow her brow. She doesn't mean to, but she shifts towards me very slightly. I take that to mean that my smile worked.

I'm in, I think.

"So I just say the word, and you back off?" she asks, keeping things light.

"Sure. I'm hoping you won't, though. Only to spare me the embarrassment." I put my hand over my heart, but stop shy of giving her a pleading face.

She seems to take that at face value, nodding.

"Alright. Which one is she?" she asks, looking around the party.

Shit. I should've been prepared for this. I scan the crowd, looking for someone who looks vaguely like Emily.

"Uhhh... she's over there," I say, nodding to a pretty,

skinny blonde by the exit door. "In the black romper thing."

"Ah," she says, nodding. "She's pretty."

I pull a face, and she goes pink.

"Sorry," she says. "I would ask why you guys aren't an item anymore, but I don't want to pour salt on the wounds."

"You can make it up to me, I'm sure," I say with a smile.

Her eye roll is particularly epic. My smile turns into a grin. I take a sip of my beer, which is pretty stale and warm by now.

I look over my shoulder to see what Mason is doing, but he's nowhere to be seen. *Fucker.*

When I look back, she is frowning at her phone screen again, her brow puckered. Shit, she is losing interest again. Why the fuck did Mason have to pick her?

I need a new approach.

"Hey, what's so interesting on your phone?" I ask.

She looks up at me. "An email from my boss. I'm a lawyer, and my boss is a little verbose. Try as I might, I can't make heads or tails of this email."

I cock my head. How should I tackle this? I guess I haven't tried being blunt yet...

"Can I ask you a question?" I say.

"Sure. Ask away," she says, turning the screen of her phone off. She looks at me.

I lean in, dropping my voice low, using the full force of my dark blue eyes. "Do you have a boyfriend, or a husband?"

She blushes, the pale pink tinging her high cheekbones. "No."

"Okay. How about this, then? You put your phone away for twenty minutes, and let me be entertaining."

The pale pink spreads out to her cheeks. "Alright..." she says hesitantly.

She drops her phone into her handbag with a satisfying thunk. I grin and stick out my hand.

"Jett James."

"Cady Ellis," she says. Her handshake is firm, domineering even.

I get a mental image of me dominating her in bed, and her fighting it for every second until she's screaming my name. A lick of heat stirs my cock.

It's in that moment that I decide that I like her.

"A pleasure," I assure her. "It looks like you're done with your drink. How about we go over to the bar and get another one?"

"Oh, I don't know... I have to work tomorrow..." she says. But I can tell that she wants another drink, wants the excuse to flirt.

"Come on. One more drink," I say, offering her my hand. I wink at her. "Our relationship needs some spice."

She rolls her eyes, but allows me to guide her to the bar. I order a whiskey neat for myself, and she orders a vodka with a little soda and extra lime slices.

"And two shots of tequila," I say. "Don't even pretend that you don't want it. You're getting the shot."

Her brow arches, but she doesn't disagree. "Fine."

The bartender pours the two shots, and hands me the limes. I slide the shot glass over to her, and raise mine.

"What should we toast to?" she asks.

"To having a good night," I say, clicking my glass to hers. I shoot the liquor, which burns, but tastes so good. The lime takes the edge off, tasting sweetly sour after the tequila.

"Jesus," she says, shuttering as she bites down on her slice of lime. "I haven't shot tequila since college."

I wink at her, tucking the used lime wedge in my shot glass. "Come on, let's go over to the edge of the roof. I like to get a different perspective whenever I can."

I lead the way, and she follows me to the edge, which has been roped off with metal bars. I look over, and I'm treated to a view of a busy downtown Atlanta street corner from eight stories up. Although it's late at night, there's still a good amount of traffic, giving me the impression of a sea of red tail lights.

Cady stops beside me, leaning over to peer down. I glance at her ass, which happens to look pretty damned fantastic right now, encased in the sheath of her pencil skirt.

"Everything is so small when I'm up here," she sighs.

"I think that's the tequila talking," I say, wiggling my eyebrows.

She glances at me. "Yeah right."

She turns away from the view, leaning her elbows over the topmost metal bar. I mimic her position, and notice that I'm half a foot taller than her. It's a lot less than the height difference on the girls I'm used to dating, but still pleasing.

She sneaks a glance at me, then sips her drink.

"What do you do?" she asks.

"I'm a sports agent," I say. "But I used to be a professional baseball player."

Her eyebrows fly skyward. "Really?"

"Yep. I was a center fielder for the Atlanta Braves for three years."

"Why don't you still play for them?" she asks, cocking her head to one side.

I make a face. "I tore my rotator cuff. The team doctor took one look at my shoulder and said I needed surgery. That was pretty much it, as far as my career went."

"Jesus. I'm sorry," she says, eyeing my shoulders. I can feel that calculation again, her steely grey eyes scanning me as they try to do some kind of math.

"It's fine. I get to do something I love, so I can't really be upset about it." I take a sip of my whiskey, and enjoy the burn as I swallow. "What do you do again?"

"I'm a lawyer. A civil litigator, to be exact. I work for Hansen & Felder."

"I'm afraid I don't know anything about the law."

"We're one of the top firms in the city," she says primly.

"That sounds fancy," I tease. She looks at me and chuckles.

"Yeah. It's not very romantic," she admits. Her phone starts buzzing in her purse, very insistent. "Ugh, like this. It's ten-thirty on a Friday night, and I'm still getting phone calls."

"Tell them you went to bed early. You were feeling a little ill, and wanted to head it off." I raise my brows. "That way you're covered tomorrow, too."

Again, I can tell that she wants to take my advice, but a part of her hesitates.

"Oh, I don't know..." Cady says, wrinkling her nose.

"You know what you need?" I ask.

"Ummm, to actually go to bed early?"

"No, I think you need to dance."

"Oh, I don't know, Jett—" she says. Her body language is all kinds of reticent.

"This doesn't bode well for our relationship, Cady," I tease. "Come on, just one dance."

She makes a face at me, but allows me to take her glass from her and put it down. I take her hand in mine, noticing how dainty it seems, and lead her to an area where there are a number of people dancing.

Cady is stiff at first, her face saying "I can think of ten things I'd rather be doing than this." She moves as if she's carved from wood, and barely touches me.

That won't do at all.

I gently turn her around, bring her body against mine. The music pulses, and we move with it. Slowly at first, then more frenetic, until she's all but grinding on me.

Fuck yes, I think. *God, she feels good.*

Cady surprises me by turning around, slipping her arms around my neck, and kissing me. I'm a little caught off guard at first, but her lips are soft and sweet. Inviting.

The sensation goes straight to my cock, and I am fucking rock hard in an instant.

I take over the kiss, dominating her lips, snaking my tongue against hers. She tastes fucking amazing, like fresh mint and vodka. I could drink from her lips all night long.

She pulls back, practically panting. "Do you want to go back to my place? I don't live far."

Oh, fuck *yes*. I really, really do.

Only Mason is suddenly in my head, ruining everything. *It's too easy to just go home with a girl and never see her again.*

I stare down at her, still tasting her on my lips. It would be great to take her up on her offer, to just go to her place and fuck her until the sun rose. But something about her won't let me do that.

Is this what being a gentleman is like? I wonder.

"You know, there is nothing I would like better than to take you home, make you scream my name over and over till you're hoarse," I whisper, leaning in close. "I don't think that would be good for our relationship, though. I can't take you home, we haven't even had our first date."

She immediately turns red as a beet. "I… I… I should go…"

Cady takes her phone out of her purse, turning away. My arm shoots out and I grab her, pulling her back.

"You're not leaving without my number," I say. "Don't even try."

I pluck her phone from her hand, ignoring the open-mouthed look she's directing at me. It's the work of a few seconds to put my name and number in, and then I call myself. My phone starts blaring "Swimming Pools" by Kendrick Lamar, and I wink at her.

"I have your number now," I taunt her. I hand her phone back.

"Ugh, good*bye*," she says, turning away again.

I can't resist the chance to grab her and spin her back against me, to press my hips against her and claim her mouth once more. Her fingernails dig into my chest, but I can tell she likes a little dominance.

I release her, my fingers itching to slap her on the ass. That pencil skirt is practically begging for it, honestly.

"Now you can leave," I say with a grin.

I wish I had a photo of her expression, of the outrage mixed with carnal interest. Outrage won, and she sneered, turning on her heel. I watched her flee, as fast as she could on those tall high heels.

I crack my knuckles, thinking that I should've just taken her home, Mason be damned.

I move towards the exit, adjusting my bulge in my pants, and look around. Mason and Alex are nowhere to be found. *How typical.*

I take the stairs slowly, and think of Cady. Her red sweater, her pencil skirt, her high heels.

Yeah, women are pretty much all the same... But at least someone has caught my interest.

I smile as I head downstairs.

CADY

I open my eyes and groan. It's not just the morning, it's full on sunshine city in my room right now. Milo, my stray-turned-cuddle-fiend, purrs and rubs his chin against my fingers.

"Fuuuuuuck," I say, rolling over. Milo looks at me with pure judgment in his one remaining blue eye. The other one has long since been stitched up, and healed over. He's a Siamese mix, and snobby as hell for someone who I rescued from a dumpster outside my house.

Milo doesn't care that I went out drinking last night. He rubs his chin against my hand again, meowing in his raspy voice, demanding pets. I scratch the top of his head, and he bursts into a full purr, rumbling happily.

"You're the worst," I say to Milo. He climbs up onto my chest, his weight slight. Even after having him for a year, he hasn't ever gotten any bigger than ten pounds. "I do not appreciate you at *all*."

He kneads the blanket on my chest a bit, then hops off me. He heads to the end of the bed, looking back at me with anticipation. I heave a sigh at his attempt to lure me into the kitchen, to feed him some canned food.

"You have plenty of dry food," I say, scowling.

I roll over and sit up, making a pathetic noise. At the moment, I feel every one of my thirty three years, and then some. I really am not twenty years old anymore, and I have the hangover to prove it.

I pull on a t-shirt over my panties, the first step of many to get this day started. I check my phone and see that it's only nine. Normally I would completely panic, but I know that I have the day off.

Well, maybe not off-off, but I planned on working from home today anyway. I glance at my email for a second, then heave a disgusted sigh and turn the screen off. There are a dozen new emails, a dozen voicemails, and two dozen texts waiting for me.

I pad across the bare cement floors of my loft apartment, shooting a glare at the two banks of floor-to-ceiling windows that provide amazing light. Aside from my bedroom, the apartment has a home office, a spare bedroom, and a huge kitchen-slash-living space. I paid a king's ransom for it, but I can't complain much. Not even when there's too much sunlight.

I pee, panties around my ankles, door open, and eyes shut against the light, and I force myself to think. My brain isn't really working though, so I strip my clothes off and turn on the shower. The steam starts to build up, caught in between the cool, dark tiles and the glass door.

I lean my head against the glass for a moment. I think about last night, and everything comes back in a rush.

The roof. The party. Jett.

God, I couldn't even leave with grace. Not without Jett pulling me into his arms, kissing me, making me blush. He's so tall, with near-black hair done in an undercut. A red plaid shirt and jeans that fit, and boots. Dark blue eyes, a royal blue. He had a serious beard, which I'm very into.

Oh, and his tattoos…

He's tatted on every visible inch of skin, from his neck to the unbuttoned vee at his neck, down to his fingers. I bite my lip as I slip into the shower. God, I will think about those tattoos when I get bored and lonely, that was for certain.

I stand under the shower for longer than I should, thinking about the reasons I can't have a man like Jett in my life. Oh, there are so many reasons.

One, I don't have the time to devote to a real relationship. I have a serious job, and most guys can't appreciate a woman who works as hard as I do.

Two, I don't want to deal with the games that come part and parcel with dating a handsome guy. They are so much frickin' work.

And third, I want a baby. No, I *need* a baby, stat. And none of the bs and drama of a baby-daddy, either.

I pour some shampoo in my hair, and lather it up. I know that I seem career-obsessed, but I woke up six months ago with this *urge*. Babies started suddenly seeming cute to me, out of the blue. I found myself lingering at baby-centric window displays, and laughing at funny baby videos on Facebook.

Then I had a close friend have a baby, a little girl. It was the first time that I held a baby, smelled a baby's head. For the first time, I started seeing myself as more than just the doting aunt. I wondered if it was possible that I might want a baby.

Since then, I've started seeing babies absolutely everywhere. Not only that, I've been to see the gynecologist and the fertility specialist. Once I found out that I was physically capable of having a child, I became a little obsessed.

Can you blame me, though? Who wouldn't want the chance to have a child, to pass on all the love and care that I didn't get as a kid? The foster care system did poorly by me, but that won't happen to my child.

I rinse my hair, growing impatient. No time to fuss over what my therapist calls my *crisis of faith in my true self*. I get out of the shower, realizing that Olive should be here soon.

Milo slinks around my feet, meowing up a storm.

"I'm not feeding you any canned food!" I tell him. "No matter how cute you are, or how much noise you make."

I hurry through the dressing and grooming, still tousling my wet hair with a towel when the door buzzes. I dash to the front and check the camera. Olive smiles up at me, her bright red hair unmistakable. I buzz her up and unlock the door.

I wander to the kitchen island to get the coffee, then move over to the kitchen counter to start the coffee maker. As I'm fussing over the settings, Olive comes bursting in. She's dressed down per my request, which means that she's wearing last year's Versace and her *third* best Louboutins.

I'm in jeans and an oversized crop top, but hey. To each her own, right?

I smile at her. She can wear whatever she wants; the girl is five feet tall, weighs next to nothing, and has a heart of pure gold.

"Hey!" she says, brandishing a pink pastry box. "Guess who brought chocolate croissants from Amélie's?"

"Oh, you are a lifesaver," I tell her. "I was just glad that we don't have to be in the office today. I've just put the coffee on."

Olive smirks. She's a kick-ass defense attorney with my firm, and paid very richly for it.

"Coffee sounds amaze-balls," she announces. "And it'll go really well with the croissants."

I take the box from her, opening the lid to inhale the yeasty goodness. I can feel Olive looking at me. She won't demand details, but the way she drums her fingertips against the kitchen counter says she *really* wants to know about last night.

I glance at her. With her pixie-ish features, her abundant freckles, and her wide-set green eyes, she is almost too adorable to keep anything from.

"How was your date with Roberto?" I ask, cocking my head to the side. Milo hops up on the counter, and I automatically shoo him off.

She motions for me to bring the pastry box to her, and selects one. "It was okay. It's only the third date, so I have nothing new to report yet."

She looks at me meaningfully, and takes a bite of her croissant.

"You want to know about last night?" I sigh.

"Omigod, I really, really do," she says, struggling to seat herself on one of the stools that are on the other side of the island.

I screw up my face. "His name was Jett, he was ridiculously hot, and he turned me down for sex."

"He *what?*" she asks, outraged.

"It was super embarrassing," I say with another sigh. "Although he did make sure he got my number…"

"Wait, did he do that before or after he turned you down?"

"Ummmm… after," I say, moving to get a couple of mugs down.

"Girl! That's pretty damn hot," she says. She takes a bite of the croissant, and moans appreciatively. "God, this is good."

"You're getting crumbs all over that slinky little black number," I point out.

She brushes the crumbs off her sleeveless chiffon jumpsuit and shrugs. "So what kind of hot was he? Describe him."

"Mmmm…" I think about it as I get out the milk. The coffee finishes, and I pour us two steaming, amazing smelling cups. "He was really tall. He had short, dark hair, and a killer smile. And he had a crazy amount of tattoos."

"Like a full sleeve?" she asks, accepting the coffee from me. "Thanks."

"Both arms were inked, his neck was inked… it was pretty damned hot."

"Nice. Well, maybe he'll actually call."

"Yeah, and maybe after that little green men will come down in their spaceship!" I say. "Oooh, wait just a second…"

I leave my coffee in the kitchen and go to grab a thick white binder from the coffee table. Milo meows pitifully, and Olive bends down and scratches him on the head.

I stare at the white binder and a nearly identical black one, trying to remember which one is full of sperm donors and which is full of paint swatches for the spare bedroom.

After a quick peek inside the cover, I bring the binder of swatches over, opening it to the first page I have marked. "You have to help me choose a paint color for the would-be nursery."

Olive pulls the book over to look at the open page, and then passes me the pastry box.

"Don't want it to go to waste," she murmurs, flipping through the pages.

I take the croissant, biting into it. I close my eyes; the taste is almost as good as an orgasm. "Ohhhh."

"I know," Olive says, without looking up. "Listen, I have a weird question. No judgment or anything, but… do the partners at our firm know that you are planning to get pregnant?"

I press my lips together in a not-quite-frown. "No."

"It's just… you know, you won't be able to work nearly as much. Sarah, you know the one in contract law? She said that her billable hours were cut in half."

She doesn't look up from the book, but I feel like this is her honest-to-god moment of truth on the subject.

"I've prepared financially, if that's what you mean." I scrunch up my face.

"No, just… I wonder if the partners will feel sort of thunderstruck when one of their top litigators announces she's preggo."

"Probably. But I can't have an old white man telling me that it's a bad idea for me to have a baby just because it's bad for his bottom line. My fertility doesn't have to conform to his timeline."

"Hmm," she says, her brow puckering. "Hey, have you had any luck with the sperm donors' binder?"

I flap my hand. "Ugh, no. I've narrowed it to like… the whole list."

She grins at that. "So selective!"

"You want to hear something crazy?"

"Always."

"I almost asked him to be a 1 night stand, just to see if… you know… he wanted to help me speed up the process a little?" I cringe as I say it.

Olive's mouth forms a perfect O. It takes a second before she can speak.

"Wait, you were just going to like… use him for his sperm?"

"Well, yeah. The fact that he was hotter than fire didn't hurt, either."

"Omigod, really? That's completely amazing. I hope you got his number."

I feel the heat rising in my cheeks. Milo jumps up on the counter again, and I pick him up, stroking his soft fur.

"Actually, yeah. I did."

Olive looks at me with a considering expression.

"Are you thinking about dating him?" she asks.

"Oh my god, no. He seems like a total player. I don't have that kind of time. Especially not if I'm going to go ahead with the sperm donor thing…"

A mischievous smile curls her lips. "So like… why don't you just skip the dating part and ask him if he wants to bang?"

"You mean… like to procreate?" I ask.

"Yeah, why not? You could tell him, or not." She pauses. "It's just a suggestion."

I roll my eyes. Milo wriggles to be let out of my arms, so I put him down. "I would have to tell the father of my baby that I was trying to get knocked up. It's only the decent thing to do, Olive."

She shrugs. "If you think so."

"I'd have to, I think. Like personally, for me. But like… how do you even bring that up? 'Hey, Mr. Sexy Man, is it cool if we don't use protection? I'm trying to get pregnant'."

Olive cackles. "I'd just get him a little buzzed and lay all my cards on the table. It would probably help if you dressed sexy…"

"Ugh, I don't know. He will probably hear the word baby and get the fuck out of there."

Olive looks speculative. "Show me a picture of him?"

I shake my head. "I don't have one."

"Do you know his name?"

"Yeah, Jett James."

"That sounds familiar. Hmmm…" She whips out her phone and types something, scrolling through a few pages. "Wait… is this him?"

She turns the phone screen toward me, and Jett is splashed across it.

"Yep, that's him," I say.

"Dude! He's fucking hot! And he was a baseball player, that's why his name sounds familiar. Oooh, I bet he's got great genes!"

I sigh. "Olive…"

"Seriously, is he taller than you? It says that he's 6'3."

"Well, yeah… a lot taller…"

She sits up straight, as if a decision has been made.

"Okay, give me your phone."

I give her side eye. "What for?"

"You are totally making a date with this guy. If nothing else, you can bang it out and never see him again."

"Oh, I don't know…"

"Seriously? Phone, *now*," she demands.

I make an exasperated noise, then head into my bedroom to retrieve my phone. There's a message from Jett already waiting when I pick up the phone.

I think we should go out sometime soon. For our relationship. ;)

Followed by, *PS you looked fucking amazing in that skirt last night.*

I blush so hard, I'm sure that my cheeks are aflame. I carry my phone into the kitchen.

"He texted me," I say, offering Olive the phone.

She reads his texts, and lets out a whoop of joy. "Yes! You're totally going out with him, one hundred percent."

After a second of thinking, she texts him a single word. *Tonight?*

I want to punch her for hitting send without my okay,

but the three little dots appear, indicating that he's writing back.

"I can't believe you did that," I say.

"You're welcome," Olive says, clearly proud of herself.

When he texts back, I almost jump out of my skin.

Not today. But I'm free the day after tomorrow. Sometime after 8. Will that do, princess?

I pull the phone away from Olive, worrying my lip. He's already calling me pet names? I can't decide if that's hot or just too much.

"Seriously? This super hot guy is guaranteeing that he's going to show up and give you his gift. Just say yes!" she practically shouts. When I still haven't made up my mind a few seconds later, she grabs my phone.

I'll be there, Daddy. 😘

"Omigod, *really*?" I squeak. "Oh fuck. I can't believe you sent that!"

"What's the worst that can happen?" Olive says. "You're already having a baby alone. Besides, this raises a very important question."

"Does it now?" I ask, unamused.

"Yeah. What are you going to wear? Something that says, *I'm classy, but also, please fuck me.*"

"Oh, christ—" I protest, but Olive isn't hearing any of it. She's too busy dragging me to my closet.

I guess I'm really going on a date with Jett James, and soon.

JETT

I wake up early, just before the sun rises. It doesn't matter if it's raining, snowing, sleeting, or hailing. It doesn't matter what time I was out until. If I'm not in the hospital, I'm gonna get my workout in.

I push back the dark linen comforter and stretch, completely naked. Emily didn't like me sleeping nude. But after Emily left me a little over a month ago, I tried it out again. It feels so good, just your skin and the comforter, no clothes to get in the way of bliss.

I get up and head to the ensuite bathroom, not bothering to turn on any lights. In the bathroom, light is beginning to trickle in from above; some clever architect planned skylights through the whole house. The bathroom features bared cedar ceiling beams and simple white walls, which is a common theme running through out the house. The whole place was done by someone with more taste and spare time than I have, and it's really minimal.

I brush my teeth in front of the giant mirror, inspecting myself. My beard is getting a little long, so maybe I'll trim it today or tomorrow. I pause when I catch sight of the dual sink.

It's not her sink, I remind myself. It belongs to whoever takes her place.

I hurry through picking some gym clothes, and then head down to the basement. I will finish my workout with some cardio, but now it's time to pump some fucking iron in my home gym. I flip on the lights and touch a button on the wall to turn on the music. Rap blares out of the built in speakers, loud and fast.

Perfect.

I move around the machines, trying to decide where to begin. I start off easy with pecs then do traps.

After my first set of reps, I think of Emily again. I have a lot of mixed feelings about her, and about the end of our relationship. Enough that I took a long weekend off from work and went camping by myself to try to figure things out.

I camped out and lay under the stars, trying to commit to memory what exactly went wrong.

First off, Emily was probably pissed at my refusal to have her move in. Actually, I'd put off any number of things that signaled a long term commitment: getting a dog together, making vacation plans that were far in the future, even getting a family plan at the gym we both went to was too much for me.

Granted, she never really got mad anytime I just shrugged off future plans. Her mouth would thin, her eyes would narrow, but nothing that affected me directly. That's how I managed to ignore her irate behavior for three years: being deaf and dumb.

So if I was going to learn anything from my failed relationship, I needed to figure out what I wanted. I also needed to commit to it. That was really the gist of what I took from the relationship.

Secondly, I figured that Mason was right when he accused me of going for the same type over and over again. Petite blondes carrying their yoga mats were my jam. If I were honest with myself, I liked that they were generally submissive and didn't challenge me too much intellectually.

Basically, my type was the exact opposite of Cady, the girl I met the other night. I picture her, dark hair and grey eyes, taller than the girls I usually liked. She had breasts and hips, and an actual ass, not just a flat yoga butt.

And her personality is so different than anyone that I've ever dated before. She's sarcastic and brainy, and she has a high-powered job at a law firm. She can stand on her own two feet, as opposed to Emily.

Emily had a lot going for her, but she also worked at a coffee shop and couldn't live without roommates.

As I switch machines and really start to sweat, my mind starts to wander. First I think of work; I still haven't signed Bryce, and I also have a meeting at work later today.

Then I think about Mason and Alex, my two best friends. I've got work buddies, but I'm really choosy about who I spend my downtime with. Mason is allergic to commitment, a new girl every night. I can't believe he had the nerve to accuse me of only having one night stands.

And Alex… Alex seems to do well with women, but that motherfucker is so secretive. He could be fucking my mom, my sister, and my grandma, and no one would know. But whatever, he's a solid dude. He always shows up when he says he will, even if that event is my grandfather's wake.

I used to have more friends when I was in college, but they slowly fell away, pairing up and then marrying... then eventually vanishing. Mason and Alex are the only ones still standing, besides me.

Sadly, that's pretty much it for what I have to worry about. I work out, I get shit done at my job, I hang out with my friends. My life is kind of empty, if I'm truthful with myself. At thirty five, I definitely thought that I would have married by now, maybe started a family.

Actually, that was what really shocked me about Emily leaving. I remember her finding the documents I had for a trip that I'd planned to take to Macchu Picchu solo.

"You weren't planning on telling me?" she asks, throwing the documents down on me when I am lying on the couch. We've been dating for almost three years at that point, long enough for me to recognize her anger.

"Ohh... I mean, that's like, three months from now," I say, sitting up.

"What is that supposed to mean?" she explodes. She is really pissed off now, her blonde ponytail bobbing with every movement. "Seriously, how could you not tell me about this? Or... wait, do you already have a woman going with you? Omigod, are you cheating??"

"Whoa, whoa. First of all, no. Seconds of all, when would I have time?" I say defensively. "I'm just saying that... you know, it's in the future. Who even knows what will be happening then?"

She fixes me with her gaze, pointing a finger at me.

"Are you questioning what will be happening three months from now in our relationship?"

"No..." I say guiltily. She stares at me for a second, and

I start to question whether or not she can read my fucking thoughts. Because I said no, but what I meant was… maybe.

"You know what? That's it. While you're gone at work today, I'm moving my stuff out. Don't bother arguing, cause I don't want to hear it."

"Wait, Emily—"

She pounds up the stairs, and I hear a faint slam. That would be the door to the bedroom.

Fuck.

The thing is, I went to work that day. I just figured that she would do what she normally did, go on a shopping binge and work out. Then things would be okay. I sent flowers from work, which I thought was a nice touch.

Only, I got home to find the house trashed, her keys on the counter, and a note.

Don't EVER call me again.

I cringe as I listen to Kendrick Lamar, then turn off the rap. I finally head upstairs, grabbing my iPod on the way out. I head outside and start my run, with all the other rich people running early in the Buckhead neighborhood. I start the rap again, listening to Drake talking about how he's famous.

I know that things with Emily fell apart because of me. That's been made clear to me now, mostly through long nights of bitching about the whole thing to my friends. Alex and Mason listen, but they aren't afraid to answer questions either.

So here I am, a newly… alright, not-so-newly single guy, on the prowl. The other night, I was pretty charmed by Cady… despite the fact that she's not my type at all.

Blonde, petite, amenable… none of those words applied to Cady.

Maybe that's a good thing, I think. Maybe I need someone who isn't my type, at all.

I try to picture myself dating Cady, holding her hand. Marrying her, seeing her face emerge from behind that white veil. Cady in the hospital, having our baby.

I can't quite see it, but then again I've never been able to see it, not with anyone. Maybe that's why I'm still alone at this age. Maybe I just have to pick someone who I think is worth my time and energy, and commit to her.

I pick up the pace, sprinting until I can no longer form thoughts.

CADY

I make it all the way to the parking deck at work and pull into my allotted space before I lose it. I turn off my car as the hot, salty tears begin to spill down my cheeks.

The goal, of course, is not to cry at all... but if I've got to do it, this is the place. Alone in my car, in the dimness of the parking lot, I am safe. I lean forward and rest head on my arms, which are propped on the steering wheel of my Mercedes. As I cry, my tears drip down onto my lap, wetting my white silk dress.

I am crying because I just came from seeing Dr. Altman, who is my reproductive endocrinologist AKA my fertility guru. Unfortunately, no matter how nice she is, there isn't a good way to phrase my situation. I saw Dr. Altman's mouth moving, but all I heard was, "YOU ARE RUNNING OUT OF TIME, CADY!!!"

So the basics of my situation are that my egg-producing follicles have really thinned out with age. Based on some pictures of my ovaries and specifically those follicles, Dr. Altman predicts that I have three good years of fertility left.

Sitting there in the hard plastic chair of her Swedish-influenced office, I did the math. Even if I was to get pregnant today somehow, that would put me a year out from even thinking about getting pregnant again. In my head, I had this perfect family planned out, with three kids that were each two years apart.

I even have their names: for girls, for boys.

I nod my head as the doctor tries to reassure me, but I know what she's really saying.

I've run out of time.

All the years of college and law school. All the late nights trying to prove myself as a first (or second, or third) year associate. All the times I doubled up on birth control because getting pregnant would've been a disaster...

All those times come flooding back as I walk out of Dr. Altmans office. She squeezes my elbow and says for the final time that it's going to be okay. I find myself wondering how often she says that to patients as I make my way through her foyer.

I get in my white Mercedes, shading my eyes against the glare of the sun, wincing a bit at how hot the seats are. I know I'm in shock. It just takes a while before it catches up to me. Twenty minutes, in fact.

So now here I am, searching my glovebox for the packet of tissues I keep there. I find them and pull one out, wiping snot and tears all over the thin piece of tissue.

What am I supposed to do with that information, exactly?

It's not like I can go back a few years, sort of unwind the clock. That isn't an option.

The only thing I can really do with the news is hurry and get pregnant. Scratch that, hurry and find a stable guy with great genes who wants to get married and have kids and *then* get pregnant.

I sink back in my seat, really bawling now. The kind of crying where I'm hiccuping and trying to breathe and cry at once, and failing at it.

Someone knocks on the window, a light *clunk-clunk* sound. I swear, I jump so hard I'm halfway out of my seat, heart racing. I furiously wipe at my face for a second before I hear a voice, distorted a little by the window.

"It's Olive," she says. "Are you alright?"

I release my breath in a gust, and squint at her. She looks back at me, concerned.

"What are you doing out here?" she says, gesturing to the darkened parking deck.

I reach over and press the button to unlock the doors, and gesture for her to get in. She runs around to the other side of the car, her Manolo Blahniks click clacking on the pavement. She gets in, her long red hair lying perfectly over a skin-tight floral sheath dress.

I feel like a sodden mess next to her, which drives me to tears again.

"Oh, omigod!" Olive exclaims, moving to embrace me. "Come here."

I let her, bending awkwardly over my center console. I make it a point not to get any of my tears on her surprisingly soft dress, holding my face a little away from her as she hugs me. I don't let it get out of hand, though. No sobbing and hiccuping.

As soon as my tears dry, I push away, ready to regain whatever is left of my dignity. Olive finds the tissues and hands me one, and I do my best to mop up my face. I hadn't considered my makeup until this moment, but I'm sure my mascara and eyeliner look horrendous.

"Are you okay?" Olive asks, putting her hand on the

back of my shoulder. She squeezes a little, reminding me of Dr. Altman. Is that the universal response to a woman's tears or something?

I clear my throat. "I'm fine. It's just… I just got back from the fertility doctor."

"Omigod. You're… infertile??" Olive's expression is worried, and she whispers the word infertile.

"No, not exactly," I say, shaking my head. "She just put a very definitive time clock on things. If I want a baby, I have to start *now*."

"Well… isn't that the point of going to a fertility expert?" Olive's face scrunches. "I thought you were ready to start!"

"I just… I think I was ready to start like… looking at paint swatches for the nursery, or buying a baby name book. Not getting knocked up, not quite yet. But now, I don't have much choice. My stupid egg-producing follicles aren't really interested in hearing anything else."

I sniff, and gesture for the pack of tissues. She hands them to me with a frown.

"Jeez, I'm a year older than you. Maybe I should go get my follicles checked," she says. "I've really never considered not being able to have kids before."

I blink at her. "I'm sorry, I didn't mean to get you wrapped up in my baby fever."

She smiles, waving my concern off.

"It's no big deal. We are talking about you, aren't we?"

I let out a shaky breath and sit back in my seat.

"Yeah. I guess… I don't know. I guess I have to go through with being artificially inseminated now."

"Or you could just have a one night stand and hope for the best," Olive speculates. "Oooohhh, or! You can ask someone to be your baby daddy. You know, draw up a bunch of legal papers that make him not accountable."

"Yeah, but then I would have to find someone and actually ask them. I'm not really in the business of meeting tons of guys," I say.

"Umm, you have a date with a super handsome guy tomorrow night, duh. You don't get a lot more easy than that. Just ask him!"

I give Olive the most disgusted look I can manage. "Yeah, right. I'll just ask Jett to be my sperm donor. I'm sure he will love that."

"Why not? What have you got to lose?"

"Ummm my dignity, for starters."

She makes a pppppffftttt noise that sounds like a straight up fart. "Do it. Your egg follicles say you should. Look, stop making that face, stop reacting, and just think about it for a second. Weren't you the one who said that he probably wasn't looking for a commitment?"

I pause, twisting my fingers in my lap. She is right, I did say that. "Well, yeah."

"So… just ask him! See what he says. If nothing else, it's good practice for when you ask the man who eventually becomes your baby's biological father."

I exhale. "I don't know."

Olive glances at her slim gold watch. "Alright. I have to get to court, and you no doubt have a ton of work to do. Just think about it, okay?"

"Alright. Hey, thanks for knowing that I was panicking in here."

She laughs, the sound a bit like a braying donkey. I smile at her.

"I didn't know you were panicking, I just thought you might have a tampon in your car."

I grin. "I do! Check the glovebox."

She opens the glovebox and fishes around, to some success. She waves several shiny blue wrappers at me.

"Got them! Thanks."

"I really have to go," she says, opening the door. "Think about what I said, though! Jett James would make an excellent baby daddy."

I try to retort, but she closes the door on me, click-clacking away. I stay in my car for a little while longer, considering it.

JETT

I shift on the worn oak bench I'm sitting on, glancing out at the street through the window. I move the heavy drape aside, giving me a better view, but it doesn't help. An older woman approaches the bar and pulls open the door.

I lean back with a sigh. I can admit it, I'm anxious for Cady to show up.

Inside, the decor is all brocade and velvet, the lighting dim. It's a hook-up bar, you can tell by the Victorian furnishings and the price of the drinks.

I sip the old-fashioned I've been nursing, draining the last watered down drops. I check my watch, but she's not even supposed to be here yet.

Why did I decide to come here early? I ask myself for the third time.

But I know why. Why do I do anything? Because I'm a horny prick, that's why.

I glance out the window, and this time I see Cady. I whistle to myself.

Hot damn.

The first time I saw her, she was dressed up, probably for work. Tonight, though, she's wearing this incredible red sheath dress, leaving her arms bare. I slide my gaze up and down her figure, particularly the fucking miles of legs she's showcasing.

She doesn't see me when she comes to a halt outside. I take a moment to glance at her patrician features, her arched nose, plump lips, and high cheekbones. She runs her hand over her hair, which is tucked neatly back.

She really is so fucking beautiful. I go ahead and just adjust where my cock lies in my jeans, because it's going to want to stand at full attention soon.

Cady runs her hands down her dress, smoothing it. I see her take a breath, and then she pulls the front door open. I swivel a little, so that she can't tell that I was staring at her through the window.

"Hey," I say when she spots me. I stand up. "You made it."

She blushes and stands beside me. "I did."

"How about a hug? It's important to keep touch a part of our relationship," I joke.

A faint pink tinges her cheeks, but she opens her arms to my embrace, pressing her body against mine. She's so much smaller than I am, almost delicate in my arms. That thought leads me to thinking of what she would look like under me, or on top of me, moaning my name.

My cock comes to full attention. I release her and step back quickly.

"Here, come sit. We have a waitress…" I tell her, shepherding her to my little corner booth with one hand on the small of her back. I look around, and signal the waitress.

The fashionable young woman serving us comes over. She's got curly blonde ringlets, a black leather dress, and some rather interesting tattoos.

If I wasn't so busy trying to fuck Cady, I would sure as shit be talking to her.

"You need to see a menu?" she asks Cady.

I see Cady take the waitress in, but I can't read any reaction. *What is she hiding?* I wonder.

"I'll have a vodka and soda with extra lime," Cady says.

"I'll have another old-fashioned," I say with a smile.

As the waitress heads to the bar, I see that look on Cady's face again. The same calculating look as before, only this time it's about the interaction I just had with the waitress. I'm not sure what she's thinking, but I'd rather not risk it.

I need some questions, to distract us both.

"Alright. Quick facts about me," I say. Her dark grey gaze is on me now, so intent that it almost burns.

"Oh?" she says, arching a brow.

"Yes. I was born in Asheville, North Carolina. My parents are a contractor and a school teacher. I have one brother, who is younger by two years." I pause for a moment. "I'm thirty five years old, and I think I already told you what my job is."

"Yes, you did," she says, leaning back against the bench. She sweeps a lock of raven hair behind her ear. I think to myself that she looks like a model, with her red lipstick and slicked back hair.

"Give me your quick facts," I suggest. "You know, so that our 'relationship' can continue."

She smiles at my use of air quotes.

"Fair enough. I was born in Santa Fe. I…" she says, then falters. "I grew up in the foster care system, bounced around from home to home. I'm thirty three, and I already told you my job too."

"An attorney, right?" I ask.

"Mmmhm. A civil litigator," she affirms.

I notice that when she shifts, she gives me a shot of her cleavage. I'm not one to complain about a thing like that, though. The waitress brings the drinks, and I don't even look at her.

I see the tiniest moment of satisfaction in her smile. *Bingo*, I think. *So you like being the center of attention, huh?*

I hide my grin behind my drink. She takes a sip of hers, leaving a perfect red lipstick mark on the rim of the glass.

"Did you hear anything out of your ex?" she asks.

My ex? I think back to last night, and then remember what I told her. I lied about Emily being there, but I doubt that Cady cares.

"Not a word. You really did me a favor," I say, moving a little closer. I'm almost touching her arm. The next step is to casually put my arm around her shoulder.

Soon.

"I'll have to remember that," she says, flashing me a smile. "For blackmail."

I grin. "Definitely. Feel free to extort anything you want from me. I'm all yours."

"Is that right?" she says, blushing prettily.

"Oh yeah. I'm a really good guy to… you know. Know," I say with a wink.

"I see. So if I asked the waitress and the bartender how many girls you've brought in here before…"

Busted. So she had noticed what type of bar this was, then.

"I plead the fifth on that one," I say, raising my right hand.

"Yeah, I get a Tinder date kind of vibe from this place. Like I wouldn't want to sit down unless I was wearing panties, just to be safe," she jokes.

"So you're wearing panties, then?" I say, grinning wolfishly. I can't help but tease her. She brings it out in me more than usual.

She looks embarrassed. "Maybe."

I casually stretch my arms, and then slide one around her shoulders and move a hair closer. Her pert breast and lush hip are touching my arm and leg. She looks up at me with those big grey eyes. Her perfectly plump red lips are a temptation.

Soon.

"Let me guess," I say. "A pair of lacy boy shorts? Or… no, I've got your number. A teeny, tiny black thong."

She blushes all the way to the roots of her hair.

"A lady doesn't talk about her undergarments in public."

I lean close to her ear, whispering. "I'll find out sooner or later, though. Won't I?"

I wish I could take a photograph of her expression in that moment. The combination of perfect shock and suppressed lust is writ large across her face.

It almost breaks my heart when she turns away, gulping her drink down. But I am a step closer to figuring out what makes her tick. I think she likes a little dirty talk, which has me even harder than before.

I relax, keeping my arm around her, and change the subject. We talk about my tattoos, and a little about our jobs.

She seems relieved, though I notice that the tension isn't gone from her body. We talk a bit, order more drinks. I tease her, and she blushes.

I like the way I can make her flush again and again. It makes me wonder about her face when she orgasms. I'm willing to bet that she has the most amazing O face.

I'm planning on finding out firsthand what it looks like, tonight.

I'm a little distracted by looking at her body as we chat. Her legs are smooth and toned, every inch that she's displaying perfect. I usually go for short women, but Cady's long legs have got me thinking of all the positions I want to put her in.

Would she ride me like a stallion, or would she like me to fuck her from behind?

And don't even get me started on her tits. She's bustier than most of the women I date, and I imagine her bare breasts are absolutely, jaw-droppingly fantastic.

"I'm sorry, what did you ask? I was busy staring at you," I say, shrugging.

Cady blushes. "I asked if you had any heart disease in your family. Or genetic conditions."

I run my hand over my mouth and my beard, thinking. *Do I?*

"I don't think so, no. What's with the medical questions?"

She doesn't answer my question though, she just follows it up with another question.

"Umm. Are you... like, clean?" she asks, her face burning bright red. "I mean, have you been tested recently for STIs?"

This is the first question she's asked that has made me feel a little weird. I give her a suspicious glance.

"Why?" I ask flat out.

She puts her hand on my biceps in a soothing gesture.

"Just tell me. A girl has the right to know who she's... maybe... doing stuff with, doesn't she?"

My brows arch. "I've been tested within the last month, and came back with a perfect bill of health."

Her face continues to burn. She bites her lip for a second.

"Okay. Ummm... I want to ask you something," she says, her words hurried. I open my mouth to say something, but she stops me. "No, let me finish. I understand if it's too much, but... I'm trying to get pregnant."

"Whoa... what?" I say, taken aback. "You're... what?"

"I'm trying to ask you to... you know... be my sperm donor. Except I want..." She has to stop, burying her face in her hands for a second. "This is way harder than it should be."

"Are you asking me to... are you asking if I will get you pregnant?" I say. The words sound super weird coming out of my mouth.

"Yes!" she says, her words still coming out in a rush. "I can skip the whole fertility clinic thing if I find someone... someone that I like enough."

I withdraw my arm from where it was resting around her shoulders and rub the back of my neck. What am I supposed to say to that?

"I don't know..." I manage. "I just... I don't know."

"Listen," she pleads, putting her hand on my thigh. "You know I'm a lawyer. You like freedom? I'll have papers drawn up to make sure you stay that way. I'll make sure that the agreement is airtight."

She sees me glancing away and grows a little desperate.

"Jett, please look at me." I look at her, and she smiles. "Hi. Sorry. I'm just... you're so freaking hot, and you're healthy. You obviously have great genes. And I can only imagine that our... our sex would be... preferable to whatever cold, clinical stuff the sperm bank has to offer. I'm basically asking..." she says, turning red again. "I'm basically asking you to have unprotected sex with me."

"It's just... a lot to take in," I say uneasily.

On one hand, she's actually pleading with me to *pretty please* come in her. On the other hand, I don't fucking even know what to think about having a *kid*. Even if I wasn't responsible for giving it any of my money or time, I would… what? Just walk around, knowing it was out there?

"I know it's asking a lot. A really, really big favor. I understand if you need to think about it."

I look at her for a long moment. She's so tempting in that little red dress, with her long legs crossed. I want to experience her, to feel her plump lips wrapped around my cock, to feel her spasming around my cock. I want to see her blush red as a rose with her orgasm, see the storm passing through those wide grey eyes.

The wild side of me whispers *just do it*. But the reasonable side of me says *please PLEASE think about this*.

"Can I think about it?" I say at last.

She releases a breath, relieved. "Of course! Think it over, consult a lawyer… whatever you need."

Cady moves a little, then opens her purse. She throws a hundred down on the table. Apparently she's paying for the drinks tonight.

I've never felt like a prostitute before, but the situation is straying close to that territory now. I'm still at a loss for words.

"I'm just… I'm sort of…" I say, waving a hand.

"No need to explain. Just… you take all the time you need. You have my number," she says.

She leans close, putting her hand on my pec. She kisses me gently on the cheek. I groan and catch her lips with mine, unable to help myself after fantasizing about her all fucking day.

The kiss is sweet and gentle, just a brushing of lips at first. Her lips are softer than anything I can imagine. I deepen the kiss, flicking my tongue against her teeth. She makes a quiet noise that is one part keening, one part animal lust.

I swear, that sound has me rock hard in seconds.

She opens for me, and my tongue sweeps the inside of her mouth. Jesus, she tastes sweeter than fucking candy.

I feel her push against my chest, and reluctantly let her go. We stay like that for a second, just looking into each other's eyes, trying to read whatever is there.

Then she bites her lip and wipes at my lips with her fingers. "I'm afraid I've gotten red lipstick on you."

"I wear it like a badge of honor," I joke.

Cady smiles and scoots away, then gets up.

"I'll be waiting for your call," she says. "Goodnight."

"Night," I say.

I watch her walk out of the bar, and then I watch out the window. She cuts quite a figure on the darkened street, an elegant lady in red.

I sit back with a sigh. What the fuck just happened?

I've made plenty of propositions. Hell, I've even been asked for sex a few times.

But never in my thirty five years of life have I been asked *to get someone pregnant*. That, I swear, is totally and wholly unique.

I get up and leave a few minutes after Cady, my brain working overtime.

Yes, there is Cady. I have a pretty good feeling about her. That lust could be its own reward, honestly.

But what she's asking? For me to create a life? That's serious shit.

I have a lot of thinking to do about Cady and her proposition.

CADY

By Friday, I've given up on Jett completely. I get home around eight at night, carrying a huge stack of legal briefs. I'm completely exhausted as I climb the stairs to my Midtown condo. When I get to the door, it's a struggle to shift the briefs around enough to dig my keys out of my purse and unlock the door.

I finally get inside and dump the briefs on my kitchen island. I toe off my black heels, feeling relief as my bare feet hit the cool cement. Is there anything better than taking your shoes off after a long day?

I immediately go to pour myself a glass of a nice pinot noir. Milo greets me, persistently rubbing against my ankles. I set my wine glass down and spend a minute opening a can of cat food and plating it for him. He goes nuts as soon as he hears me get the can down from the pantry, meowing his approval and pacing back and forth.

"Here," I say, sitting the plate on the floor. He comes over and starts chowing down immediately, and I stroke the silky top of his head. "What are you going to do when you're not the only one that I'm taking care of in this household? Hmm?"

I take a sip of the wine, closing my eyes and leaning back against the kitchen counter. The bright notes of black cherry, berry, currant hit my tastebuds.

Swishing the wine around a bit in my mouth, I set the glass aside. It's definitely time to change.

As I head into my bedroom, I'm already unbuttoning my white silk dress shirt, pulling it from my rust-colored wool pencil skirt. I head into the small walk-in closet, unzipping my skirt and stripping down to my polka dot thong and matching bra.

What the hell, those can go too. Standing naked in my closet, putting my skirt and my shirt away, I'm just tired. I contemplate the racks of hanging clothes. Too dressy. I open my loungewear drawer, searching for something more casual.

After pulling on a pair of yoga pants and an oversized tee, I grab my glass of wine and hit the couch. The couch is new, made of a stiff pale pink linen, and it makes an odd noise when I launch myself onto it.

I sip my wine, and then leave the glass to rest on the floor. Milo comes over, having finished his food, and sniffs the glass. "I can guarantee that you don't want that," I tell him mildly.

Looking over, I can't help but see the catalog of sperm donors still sitting on my coffee table.

For some reason, looking at the book fills me with existential dread. I pick up the book and flip through it, feeling completely uninspired by the smiling men I see there. I jump up and grab my phone from my purse, checking my texts as I resettle on the couch.

There are already a half dozen texts from co-workers

about the case I'm litigating, but nothing new from Jett. I scrunch down on the couch.

I asked too much of him, and he ghosted me. Pure and simple.

I find the remote at the end of the couch and turn the tv on, watching Real Housewives. It relaxes me, oddly; it's like turning my brain off after a long day. I drink my wine and eat some leftover Thai. One glass of wine turns into three, and three turns into me opening a new bottle.

When my phone chirps, it has worked its way underneath me, startling me. I give it the stink eye.

When I check the screen, a new text message from Jett flashes.

Can we meet?

I blink. Of all the things that I expected, this wasn't one of them. Maybe he's going to tell me face to face why he can't be my sperm donor?

Biting my lip, I open the message. If that's the case, no way am I getting all dressed up and going somewhere. Besides, I'm working on my fourth glass of wine. I'm not drunk, but I'm obviously not driving anywhere either.

I'm at home, not planning on going out… but you can come here if you want, I text.

I'll be there. Text me the address, he texts back.

I'm a little surprised as I text him the address. He says that he's ten minutes away.

I look around at the Thai takeout containers, the wine glass and bottle, and the sperm donor book. Shit, I guess I should clean up. I quickly tidy the apartment, then run into my closet and try to find a less-holey tee shirt. I settle on a black off-the shoulder sweater.

I have a minute or so left, so I quickly refresh my deodorant and change the tv channel to a nature documentary.

Even though I'm expecting it, I freak a little at the sound of the buzzer. Heart beating fast, I go to the front door and check the screen.

He's there, every bit as handsome as I remember. I buzz him up, trying to remind myself that he's probably just being a gentleman. A real man would tell the woman who wants his sperm no to her face, right?

I let out a hysterical giggle just as he knocks on the door. I take a deep breath, and then go to let him in.

When the door swings open, he's there, filling up the doorway with his royal blue eyes, impeccable dark grey suit, and tattooed skin.

"Hi," he says, cracking a smile. It touches his eyes, makes them crinkle a bit.

Somewhere in the back of my mind, a voice is telling me what a bad idea it is to let him in. But I step back, sweeping a hand. I can hear my heart pounding as he comes in, and I shut the door behind him.

I'd forgotten how tall he is. I swear, my ovaries want *him.*

"Hi. Welcome," I say, tucking my hair behind my ear.

In a heartbeat, he moves toward me, pinning me up against the wall with his body. I'm too shocked to even make a sound, especially when he bends down and kisses me.

I'm not talking about some little peck, either. No. He takes my lips, teasing them a little. His beard tickles a little, sending chills up my spine. When I gasp, he uses that as an invitation to invade my mouth with his tongue, sweeping and dancing.

I become aware of the fact that he's pressed against me, so tight that I can feel his bulge where it pokes my belly.

God, yes, I think. *Take me right here, right now.*

Without warning, he ends the kiss, and steps back. I'm left off-kilter, looking up at him with confusion on my face.

His blue eyes twinkle. "I just had to double check that we have chemistry."

My fingers go to my mouth, still tingling from being kissed.

"Yeah... I think it's safe to say that we do..." I say, shaking my head. "Um... should we maybe... go into the bedroom?"

His brows arch. "Do you have the paperwork? I brought my papers from my doctor saying that I'm clean."

"The paperwork for... you getting me pregnant? No, I haven't even drafted it."

"But you can?" he asks.

"Sure, yeah," I say, frowning. I'm shaking now, the adrenaline having just hit.

He's still grinning at me like the cat who caught the canary.

"Don't look at me like that. I'm just trying to cover all my bases." He reaches inside his suit, and pulls out a sheaf of paperwork. "Here, for you. The proof that I'm clean."

I take it, uncertain what to do. "Thanks."

"I'll see you later, then," he says. He looks at me, squinting a little. "God, you have the most amazing collar bones."

I reach out a trembling hand and catch his lapel, drawing him closer. *Just for a minute*, I promise myself.

Jett allows himself to be pulled in, his grin growing wider.

This time when our lips meet, it's sweeter, slower. I reach up and put my hands around his neck. I shiver as he breaks the kiss to touch his lips to my neck, my collar bone, my shoulder.

Yes. Fuck yes.

I run my hand along his shoulder to his biceps, impressed with how muscular he is. Our lips find one another again, and I open my mouth to him. He dominates the kiss, but I give as good as I get, using my tongue as my weapon.

I force myself to pull back, and lean my forehead against his. My breathing has grown heavy in just the few moments that he's touched me.

"Paperwork?" I whisper. It comes off as a question, though I didn't mean it that way.

His whole face lights up when he laughs, and I feel the rumble all the way to my core.

"Ah yes. Paperwork," he says. He gives me a final kiss, then releases me. "Text me when you're ready. When I come back, you'd better be prepared."

"Oh yeah?" I ask, a little breathless.

He doesn't answer, he just winks. *Cocky bastard*.

He turns and lets himself out the door, and then I'm left staring at the space where he just was. I'm not going to lie, my panties are a little damp, and this was only *kissing*.

I push myself off of the wall, looking down at the papers in my hand. I grab my glass of wine from the kitchen and sink onto the couch, mulling over the last few minutes.

I decide that I know three things for certain.

One, I am so fucking hot for him, it's not even funny. Even his name is hot.

Jett fucking James.

Two, I'm going to get the paperwork drawn up as soon as possible.

And three, I am surely going to be prepared the next time he comes knocking.

That's a fact.

JETT

"So what I'm saying is…" I go quiet for a second as the cars come around our side of the racetrack, drowning out all other sound. It's a few days later, and I am at the track, trying to close the deal to sign Bryce Derrick.

No matter that I'd much rather be looking at Cady Ellis. I stifle the thought before my mind can go somewhere inappropriate and weird.

"What?" Bryce shouts.

I look at him while I wait for the noise to die down. The guy is huge, an absolute beast at 6'5. Not just that, but he's bulky, too. With his wraparound sunglasses and his oddly blockish head, he reminds me of one of the Beagle Boys from the kid's show Ducktales. Give him a red shirt and blue pants, and he would fit the part to a T.

He isn't very bright either, but that hasn't stopped the Dallas Cowboys and the Atlanta Falcons from expressing interest in him. I intend to be the agent that makes that happen for him… as soon as I can talk, that is.

The noise dies down for a minute, and I continue.

"You need someone who will be by your side, someone you can rely on to be in your corner, man."

Bryce scrunches his face. "And that should be you?"

"Yeah, dude. That should be me. I know your stats. I know where you're from, and what high school you went to. But I want to know more than that, *be* more than that. I want to be the one you call for everything."

He pushes up his sunglasses, looking at me with beady eyes.

"Where'm I from?" he asks.

"Elijay, Georgia. Home of the year apple festival."

"Uh huh," he says. He's about to say more, but the sound of the cars racing around the track is closing in again.

It's everything I can do to keep my cool. If there was ever a time for a quiet room to conduct a business deal, it would be now. But I'm outwardly placid, because the only way Bryce would meet with me at all is if I agreed to come to the Atlanta Motor Speedway.

When the cars fade out again, he looks at me. "You know my stats?"

"Yeah," I say. "I can recite them, right here, right now."

"How many intercepts?" he quizzes.

"Easy. Last season you had eight. And you had one hundred and thirty five tackles, AND twelve sacks."

He looks down, but nods.

"Yeah. You and my momma would get along. She recites my stats to everyone, even the cashier in line at the Walmart. Doesn't matter if the cashier wants to hear or not." He chuckles. "I need someone like my momma on my team. Can I trust you?"

I wait a beat, then stick my hand out. "You can count on me."

He shakes my hand, forceful in this as with everything. "Alright. Call me on Monday, and I'll come up to your offices."

"All right man, I look forward to that. Have fun out here," I say.

Bryce is already looking at his phone. Fucking millennials, am I right?

I head around the cement stands, jogging to the parking lot. Just for a little gratification delay, I make myself wait until I'm inside my shiny black Lexus before I check my phone. I have a couple texts from Cady, three hours old.

I probably should've looked at them earlier, but I wanted Bryce to feel like the attention was all on him. I swipe over to my texts.

I have the paperwork...

And, *where are you?* 🙁 *I'm waiting...*

Oh, *fuck* yes. I have never been so ready for anything as I am for Cady right now. Just thinking about her peeling off her clothing, beckoning me to come closer, has got me fucking rock hard.

I text her back, *I'm on my way, ETA 20 mins.*

I pull my car out of the parking lot, tires squealing. I floor it, grateful that I'm just missing the cutoff for rush hour traffic. Cruising down the highway, it's hard not to spend the entire time fantasizing about her... but it's better not to get in an accident and make myself later.

Besides, I tell myself, *I'm all about the delayed gratification today.*

It's come to my attention over the last few days of radio silence that I really, really need to get laid. And I could go out and get some strange, but there is something about Cady...

Well, she's ridiculously hot. That is a good half of it.

But the fact that she's asking me to fuck her with no protection? The fact that she wants it that way?

It's hard to think about anything else.

In seventeen minutes, I whip my car into a spot in her parking garage and halfway sprint to the main door. I buzz, and wait. I bounce up and down on the heels of my feet, impatient. Now that there's only a few hundred feet between me and Cady, I'm dying to get inside her apartment.

Hell, I'm dying to get inside *her*. Skin on skin, absolutely no barriers. It's not something I've done much of, but with Cady I'll be giving her what she craves... I shudder in anticipation.

I buzz again, my impatience almost getting the best of me. After another half a minute, the door finally unlocks. I charge up the steps, not minding a quick sprint as a precursor to the fucking I'm about to do.

The door is just opening when I get up there, and I push the door open. There she is, looking like pure sex in nothing but a silky white minidress, her hair long and flowing around her shoulders. She's wearing that same fire engine red lipstick as before, and it has never looked so good on anyone, I swear.

"Hey," she says shyly. "Do you—"

I shoo her back, shutting the door with a foot. She stumbles, and then recovers. I glance at the empty wineglass that she left behind her on the kitchen counter.

"Did I get here too late?" I ask.

She looks at the wine glass and flushes. "It's not... I only had a few glasses..."

"Hmmm," I say, frowning. "I'm sorry I don't conform to your schedule, princess."

She makes a face at me, and shrugs. "It's not that, really—"

"You have the papers for me to sign?" I ask.

Cady swallows visibly. "Yeah, right here."

She walks to the kitchen counter, grabbing a sheaf of papers. She comes back and hands them to me with a pen.

I skim them; I don't really have the patience for a thorough review. "Cady?"

"Yes?" she says, clearly worried.

"This isn't going to screw me over, right?" I pin her with my gaze.

"No—" she starts. I sign both copies with a flourish, and she does the same. Her handwriting is neat and precise, just like her. Rigid. Controlled.

I can't wait to mess it all up.

"Alright. Then I don't care. Less talking, more fucking." I slide my jacket off and leave it on the floor. "Come here."

"Don't you want—" she starts again, but I'm done listening.

I move over to Cady, sweeping her up in my arms. She weighs nothing as I carry her forward to the couch. I swallow the softly surprised sound she makes, kissing her hard.

I fit my lips against hers, nearly groaning when she hits the couch, her hips driving against mine. I come down on her, careful not to crush her with my weight. Her hands are everywhere, exploring, diving into the short hair at my nape.

Yes. This, this is what I've been fantasizing about all fucking week.

Her lips taste like the wine she's been drinking, sweet and bitter at once. I rear up, pulling her to a sitting position. I kneel between her thighs and start to taste every inch of her dewy fucking skin.

I hear a meow, and out of the corner of my eye, I see a little Siamese cat glaring at us. I pull back, looking at it; it stares back with one brilliantly blue eye. The place where the other should be is smooth, a faint scar marring the spot.

"That's Milo," she says, noticing that the cat has caught my attention. "He's my rescue."

I make a noncommittal sound, trying to ignore the fact that her cat is looking at me with something like hatred in his eyes. My lips move down to the supple column of her neck, pausing for a fleeting moment at the pulse point.

She mewls as I move down to her collarbone, exploring the dip with my tongue. I kiss her shoulder and then the tops of her breasts, which are peeking from the top of her white dress.

She digs her nails into my back through my shirt, and I groan. I stop for a second, grabbing both her wrists and pinning her hands at her sides. She looks at me with wide grey eyes, her dark hair wild.

"Be still," I growl at her.

She bites her lip, watching me. I kiss her again, dominating her with my mouth, my tongue moving in time with hers. Cady gets into the kiss, even bites my lip.

The pain is sharp, but I like it. What I like more is that I can smell her arousal, a faint note of excitement in the air. Running my hand down her hip and to her knee, it's only natural that I skim my hand back up underneath her skirt.

I find nothing but bare skin beneath as I brush my fingertips against her hip.

Oh fuck, she really is ready for me.

I make eye contact with her as I slowly use my palms to part her thighs. She bites her lip again, her brow puckering. The way that Cady's breath all but stops when I pull her toward the edge of the couch tells me everything I need to know.

Looking down, I push the hem of her dress up and see her pussy. It's nice and pink, carefully groomed, and laid bare before me like a feast waiting to be eaten. I can see how excited she is. It's evident in the way that her pussy is glossy and wet, in the way her clit pushes forward toward me.

Perfect.

"You have a fucking gorgeous pussy," I tell her, kissing the inside of her knee. "Everything about you is completely fucking beautiful."

Cady whimpers as she watches me bow my head in preparation. Using two fingers to spread her wide, I run my tongue ever so gently over her sensitive clit.

"Jesus! Jett…" she gasps. I like the sound of my name on her lips.

"Mmm," I say. "You taste like fucking honey."

Fuck, I'm so goddamn hard. There is some little part of me that protests the idea that she had to get drunk to have me, but I shove it down.

Her entire body trembles with need. I run my tongue over her clit again, and she moans and buries her hands in my hair. She's got a hair trigger, which I try to keep in mind as I trace the alphabet against her pussy.

Moisture seeps from her pussy, but I haven't even touched it yet. Cady gets louder and wetter as I feast on her, and my beard grows damp. She's wound tight as a spring, on the verge of coming.

I should stop. I should make her beg for it. I should, at the very least, be concerned about when I get my orgasm.

But instead I slide one thick finger into her velvety core, pressing my mouth into her clit, and watch her explode all around me. I feel the tremors start in her center, watch her throw her head back and call my name.

My cock throbs, insistent, but I just help Cady ride out her orgasm with my finger and mouth.

When she slows down, I withdraw. Her cheeks are nice and dusty pink, just as I expected. When I straighten up, she kisses me, full on with tongue.

I guess she's not squeamish, then.

Cady reaches for the button on my jeans, but I stop her, shaking my head.

"No," I say.

"No?" she asks, still a little breathless.

"No. The first time I have you, you won't have half a bottle of wine in your system," I say, pushing to my feet.

She grabs the hem of her dress and pulls it down, frowning at me.

"I'm not drunk."

"I didn't say that. What I said was that you'll be sober the first time I take you." I reach down and caress her breast, pinching the sensitive nipple. "You want that, don't you?"

She gasps. "Y-yes…"

I smirk, moving my hand up to trace her delicate collar bones.

"You want me to come in you next time, no condom? You want me to fuck you with no barriers? Nothing but skin on skin?" I ask teasingly.

Cady worries her bottom lip, turning pink. "You know I do."

I continue my slow exploration, slipping the thin linen strap off her shoulder. "Say it."

"What?" she asks, confused.

"Tell me what you want me to do to you, Cady."

She blushes so red.

"I… I want you to fuck me, without a condom. And I want you to come in me," she whispers.

"You want me to knock you up?" I ask, pulling one side of the top of her dress down in slow degrees until her breast is nearly bare.

Her eyes widen. "Yes."

"Yes what?"

"Yes, I want you to…" she stops and swallows. "I want you to knock me up."

"Dirty girl," I say, leaning down for a final kiss.

I detach myself from her, wiping my beard on the sleeve of my shirt. There's still a bit of residual moisture, but I don't mind. I head toward the front door, picking up my coat.

"Wait!" she calls.

I glance back, holding back a smirk when I see how disarrayed she is. "Yeah?"

"When will I see you again?" she asks, smoothing back her wild hair. Out of the corner of my eye, I see her cat again, staring at me with the most chilling look in his eyes.

Well, eye. He's only got one. Either way, I'm petty sure he wants to kill me.

I grin anyway. "Really soon, princess. Really soon."

And then I let myself out.

CADY

It's almost five, and I'm still hungover. Will I *ever* stop doing this myself?

I'm sitting in my home office, facing a laptop and surrounded by case files. I woke up bright and early as usual, but my hangover has gotten progressively worse throughout the day. Ever since I turned thirty years old, this is a thing that's been happening.

I stare at my laptop for a few more seconds, then raise my carton of coconut water to take a sip. It's empty, which makes me groan.

I stand up and snap my laptop closed, heading into the kitchen. I'm wearing a pair of loose, dark grey harem pants and a white t-shirt under an oversized dark blue button up. The sleeve of the button up gets caught when I open the refrigerator to grab another carton of coconut water.

My temper flares and I shake loose of the fridge, scowling. Milo jumps down from his favorite spot by the window, on a special raised, heated bed I got for him. He comes over and I sit down, giving him some affection, scratching his head. He loves it, and starts climbing into my lap and purring. I'm reminded why I love him so much.

"You are really, ridiculously cute," I tell him, nuzzling his soft fur.

He jumps off my lap and sprawls out on the floor, rolling over to show me his belly. He's like a dog in that way, except that I pet him a little and then he gets excited and attacks my hand. I play with him a little longer, and then he gets bored of me. He walks away and licks his paw, then looks up at his window perch in anticipation.

"Yeah, I know where you'll be," I tell Milo.

The door buzzes, unexpected. I leave my coconut water in the kitchen and go to check the screen next to the door.

Olive beams up at me, and shows off some kind of food in a big brown paper bag. I haven't talked to her at all today, but I buzz her up.

I unlock the door and then wander back to the kitchen, sitting in one of the island stools.

"Hey!" Olive says, out of view. I hear her close the door behind her, then see her bright red locks and tiny frame appear.

As usual, she's dressed to kill, in a pale pink cropped silk pantsuit, a slightly darker trench coat, and barely there silver stiletto sandals.

"Jesus, you look like a million bucks," I grouse as she sets down the food.

"Hello to you too," she says, eyeing me. "You look... tired."

I scowl at her. "You can say it. I look like the bottom of a shoe that's been worn in Wal-Mart for several years."

She laughs.

"You're so dramatic. Cheer up, I got us Chinese from

that place we like in Decatur." When I start to get up, she waves me back down. "Sit, sit. I got chopsticks."

Milo smells the food and comes to investigate, running his skinny body against the corners of the kitchen island. Olive unpacks six different Chinese takeout cartons, which makes me smile.

"What did you get? Or should I say, what didn't you get?"

"Funny, funny lady!" she exclaims, taking off her coat and draping it over the couch. "I got Szechuan tofu and chicken, two really good dumplings, those green beans you like, and beef with broccoli. I don't like having to choose one thing, you know? Besides, don't even pretend that you won't eat this for a whole week. I know you."

I pick up a pair of chopsticks, snapping them apart. Then I set in on the first container, which happens to be one of the dumplings. I take a bite and I'm immediately reminded of why I love that place; it's so fresh, while still managing to be soul food.

Especially for my hangover.

"Omigod," I say rapturously around my second bite. "It's so friggin *good*."

Milo meows pitifully, as if I didn't feed him half an hour ago. I wave a chopstick in Milo's direction. "Ignore him, I just fed him."

Olive nods, sitting down beside me. She digs through the beef and broccoli with her own chopsticks. She grins. "Thank god for this place."

I move on to the green beans and the Szechuan chicken, taking Olive's approach of eating a little of everything.

"So, you're hungover?" Olive asks. I shoot her a look. "What? I'm just asking. Making conversation."

"Yeah. I texted Jett yesterday, but I didn't hear anything back for a few hours, so... I had a pity party."

"Oh, that sounds like a hot mess," she says, abandoning the beef and broccoli for the dumplings. "So you drank a bottle of pinot and crashed? That's not fun."

"Actually..." I say, then stop to take a particularly appetizing bite.

"Don't leave me hanging!" she says, elbowing me. "Jeez!"

"Mmm, sorry. I was saying that actually, my night took an interesting turn. Jett came over..."

Olive turns to me, her eyes wide. "He *did*?"

"Yep. He came over, we made out, he went down on me like a fucking rockstar..."

"Shut. UP."

"Nope. Then, get this. He refuses to have sex with me for the first time when I'm not stone cold sober, talks dirty to me, and leaves. It was *extremely* confusing." I throw my chopsticks down.

"It sounds hot, though!" Olive says. "Does he have any cute friends?"

I roll my eyes. Milo meows, and I bend down and give him a pat.

"I'm not sure that we have that kind of connection. I can't exactly see myself going on double dates with him."

"I'm just saying," she says, sliding off her stool. "If he mentions anything..."

I grin at her. Olive is doing perfectly fine on her own. She's got six boyfriends *that I know of*, all of them know about each other, and all of them are — by some miracle — totally fine about it.

"Yeah, you'll be the first one I call." I stand up and start putting the leftovers straight in the fridge.

"You got that right." Olive looks at me smugly.

My phone chimes, and I'm a little too quick to check it. It's Jett, just as I hoped.

What are you doing right now?

"What, is loverboy already calling?" she says.

I worry my bottom lip, suppressing a smile. "Maybe."

Nothing much, I text him back. It isn't very creative, but I only have so many brain cells to spare at the moment.

"Well, don't let me stop you. I have a date with… actually, I'm not sure which man. I'll have to look at my phone," she says. She pulls her phone out of her pocket. "Michael."

I chuckle. "As long as you're safe and happy."

"Ohhh, I can't believe you're going to be the bad one of the pair of us. All that rugged manliness… unprotected." She wrinkles her nose. "Makes me jealous."

Do you want something to do? he texts. A second later, I get his follow up question. *Or someone?*

I flush the exact color of Olive's outfit, a dusty rose. Just thinking about last night makes me crazy horny.

"All right, let me get out of here," Olive says, going to pick up her coat. "Call me tomorrow?"

"Of course," I say, giving her a quick hug. "Thanks for showing up with food. I needed it."

"Later!" she says. I hear the door open and close, but I'm focused on my texts.

There is nothing I'd like more, I respond. *My place?*

Be there in 15, he answers.

I look down at my clothes and realize that I have only a few minutes to get ready. I sprint to my closet, opening the lingerie drawer. I pluck out a matching set of barely there black panties and a bra, then dig through the drawer for a teddy made of rose-colored silk.

I dress as quickly as possible, quickly brush my teeth and put deodorant on, then light a few candles. The sun's not yet set, but the candles will burn for awhile. In my mind when Jett is done, the sun will be down, and we'll need the candles to see.

The sound of the door buzzer goes off before I'm ready. My heart takes flight within the walls of my chest. I buzz him up with barely a glance at the security screen.

When he knocks, I unlock the door with a trembling hand. The door swings open, and there he is, filling up my whole damned doorway. He's wearing a light grey flannel shirt, black jeans, and black Doc Martens. I take a good long look at his short, black hair, his sparkling eyes just the color of sapphires, his big, muscular frame. I look at his lazy grin; it's the look of a man who knows he's getting some action tonight, without a doubt.

"Do I pass inspection, princess?" he drawls.

I bite my lip, stepping back without a word. He does pass inspection, but I'm not about to tell him that.

Jett steps inside and closes the door, then moves toward me like a cat stalking his prey. He's busy looking at me just as I did him, and I can feel his eyes on my naked skin.

"I see you wore something pink. Just the color of your cheeks after you climax," he says.

My hands fly to my midsection, fingers knotting. For the life of me, I cannot think of the right thing to say.

"Maybe," I say with a delicate shrug.

He closes in on me, then walks past me at the last second, heading toward the bedroom.

"Not maybe," he says as he pushes the door open.

I watch him as he takes in my bedroom, furnished simply with an large four-poster bed, two end tables, and a bookcase. He heads further inside, and I watch him as he checks the strength of one of the posters, and then looks back at me.

"I saw your face last night, when I was eating your

pussy," he says, sitting down on the bed. He leans back on his hands. "It was exactly the color that you're wearing. A nice touch, if it was on purpose."

My mouth forms a tight line as I follow him into the bedroom. I'm not prepared for this, whatever game he's playing. He's put me off balance.

"It wasn't," I say, crossing my arms over my torso.

He ignores me, continuing on as if he hadn't heard me.

"I like your bedroom. It's nearly spartan," Jett says. "There is one thing that would make me like it more, though."

He's quiet after that, provoking me into a response. I cock my hip.

"Oh? What's that?"

"Yesterday, I made it all about you. And while I do love going down on you, there is something else I want." He leans forward, his eyes sparking with sudden intensity. "I want today to be all about me. And I want you to start by showing me what you do all by yourself in here."

I look at him, my brow lowering. "What?"

"I'm asking you to show me your vibrator," he says, smirking. "I know you have one."

My breath hitches, my heart starting to clatter in my chest again. He wants *what?*

"My... my vibrator?" I stammer, unsure.

"Yes. I want you to get it out of whatever drawer you hide it in, and I want you to put on a show for me." He sits back, crossing his arms to mirror my own. "I want to watch you touch yourself."

"I—" I gasp, startled. "I can't do that! You're— you're practically a stranger!"

He smiles, showing two rows of perfect white teeth. "Am I? After all, you asked me for something totally inappropriate."

I break into a sweat and get goosebumps on my arms.

"I know, but—"

He cuts me off. "Are we going to have mind-blowing, out of this world sex? Or should we just do it in missionary, get it over with? Because I know what kind of sex I have time for, and it ain't some bland fucking vanilla shit."

I hold my breath. He's got me there; I hadn't imagined much past the fact that we would both be in the same room. If he was going to do this more than once, which would probably be required, I was going to have to give a little.

"Okay," I say, my voice shaking a little.

"Okay?" he asks, his brows rising.

I walk over to the little bedside table closer to him, pulling out the drawer. I rustle around for a second, producing my vibrator. Well, it's one of two, but he hardly needs to see the one that's shaped like a dick. I brandish the smaller one, a little pink number meant for clitoral stimulation.

"Here it is," I say tightly.

Jett actually looks pretty impressed.

"I thought you were going to shut me down, say vanilla works for you." He grins. "Now I'm actually going to enjoy myself. Take my shoes off and everything."

Fuck! I could've gotten away with not doing this? I steam silently.

I glare at him as he moves to the edge of the bed, unlacing his Doc Martens. I put the vibrator on the bed, then move to pull my panties off.

He straightens up, reaching over and plucking the panties from my hand.

"I knew you wore a thong," he says, looking pleased with himself. I ignore him, climbing on the bed, resting on my knees.

"Kiss me," I order him. "I need a little help, to get me started."

He twists around, taking my mouth without further guidance. Jett's lips are firm yet sensual against mine, his tongue writhing, toying with me. Dominating my mouth. Reminding me of just how good it felt yesterday when he ate my pussy.

Just the thought is enough to make heat bloom in my core. I feel a tendril of moisture slither from my center, and it feels fucking *dirty*. To my surprise, he breaks off the kiss and tugs up the hem of my teddy.

"Off," he says simply.

I shift, helping him take it off. It leaves me bare, naked before him except for the bra. He kisses my collarbone, and my breasts through the material. Jett's arms encircle me, and he unhooks and removes my bra.

He takes a second just to look at my nude body. I squirm a little, wanting to put my hands over my breasts, but he isn't having it.

"Stop that," he commands, his voice raised.

My heart is hammering; it seems so loud that I am sure he can hear it. He looks for another few seconds, then moves close to kiss me again.

His kiss is magic, or at least it seems that way. I forget about my loud heart, about my shyness, about everything except for the kiss. He palms one of my breasts, drawing the pebbled peak to a hardened point. When he pinches my nipple, I gasp. It feels fucking great; moreover, it feels like there is a line connecting my nipples to my pussy.

Jett picks up my vibrator, and eases me into a reclining position. *It should be so wrong*, I think. *Touching myself in front of a stranger. But Jett is so fucking hot, and he's kissing me, and touching me...*

He pushes my vibrator into my palm, kissing my neck.

He hits the sweet spot on my neck, the place that makes my toes curl, and sucks softly.

"Ahh," I whimper. "Fucking hell, Jett."

He chuckles, sucking a little harder. My eyes threaten to roll back in my head. All I can think is *unnnngggggghhhh unnnnh unnnnnnghhhhhhhhhh.*

When he parts my legs, I'm ready for him. No, I'm beyond ready.

Fuck me, already. Plant your seed in me. Fill me to the fucking brim.

"You need this," he whispers. He touches my hand to remind me that I'm clutching the vibrator.

Clumsily, I turn the vibrator on the lowest setting. Jett guides my hand down, and he spreads my pussy lips with his enormous fingers. I close my eyes, intending to concentrate. With the first touch of the vibrator, I nearly shoot off the bed, quivering.

"Fuck," I whisper.

"Are you sensitive?" he asks.

"Yes," I bite off.

I feel him move away from me for a minute, and I open my eyes a crack. He's peeling off his shirt to reveal an amazing physique, absolutely astonishing abs.

"Keep going," he urges. "Don't stop."

I touch my clit again, feeling a moan building in my chest. He unbuttons and shucks his jeans, leaving him in a pair of black boxer briefs. As he comes back toward the bed, I get a glimpse of his cock's size through the stretchy fabric, and I'm fucking impressed.

He looks like that and he's packing a python? Holy shit, for once in my life I sure can pick a man.

Looking at his bulge makes my core tighten with want. He returns to my side, lying down and propping himself up with one arm. Jett puts his hand on my inner thigh, then trails two fingers up to my center, teasing.

"Please," I say, moving restlessly.

"Please what?" he says, a smile on his face.

"Use your fingers," I beg. "*Please*, Jett."

"Like this?" he asks, circling the area around my center. He slides one long finger inside me, beckoning in a come hither gesture.

"Fuck! Yes, just like that," I say, gasping for breath.

All the sudden he withdraws, leaving me high and dry. I'm devastated for a second. I was *thissssclose*.

"It looks like fun," he says with a wicked smile. "I'm thinking that instead of you coming all over my hand, you come on my cock."

My eyes must have lit up, because he laughs. I turn the vibrator off, tossing it aside. Jett pulls his boxer briefs off, letting his cock spring free.

Holy mother of god, I think, staring openmouthed. *Look at the fucking size of his dick! Is that thing even going to fit? And... is that a piercing??!*

His cock is a python, that I wasn't wrong about. It's perfectly pink, as thick around as my wrist. His cock is long, too, the tip nearly touching his belly button. And I see a glint of a Prince Albert piercing as the cherry on top.

Thirty-three years old, and I've never felt a Prince Albert. I blush all over again.

"Don't give me ideas," he says, using his fingertips to close my mouth for me. "Now climb on."

I don't hesitate again, rolling over and straddling his hips. He makes it easy for me, lifting me further up his body and positioning his cock at my entrance. He kisses the tip of one of my breasts, making me slick with need once more.

I wonder how many women he's done this exact move for? asks a little voice in the back of my head.

But then his cock nudges my center, and I forget everything else. As I press down, I feel a delicious stretch. Where I would normally stop, I have to slide back up and try again, because his cock is ridiculously long and thick.

"Jesus, you feel so fucking good," he says, his voice gone to gravel. "God *damn*."

He seems very focused on taking it slow, gripping my hips as I try a few times to take the whole thing. I can feel his piercing a little when I move. When I finally manage to take him to the hilt, I can see that he's broken into a sweat, because his hair is a little damp.

"You're so tight," Jett says, running his hands up my hips to my breasts. "Fucking perfect."

He tweaks my nipple a little, and that makes me moan. "Ahhhh, yes. Mmmmmm."

I start to move, slowly at first, for his benefit. Soon, though, he's encouraging me with little thrusts. The feel of him, especially when I raise myself to the top and then come shuddering down... it's almost too much.

"Fuck," he says, moving his hand down to my clit. He rubs the top of my clit with his thumb, making me clench around him. "Oh, *fuck*. God, I knew I should have masturbated before I showed up here. I'm so fucking close, Cady."

"I'm close too," I pant. "I'm so close."

"Fuck yes. I'm going to fucking come in you, skin on skin. I'm going to fill you up to the brim with my cum," he says, his eyes closing tightly.

"Yeah you are," I groan. "God, fuck me, Jett..."

He starts to really thrust now, his movements wild. The pressure of his thumb hitting my clit, the weird-but-amazing feeling of his piercing, the thickness of his cock as I move up and down...

I shatter, my whole pussy clenching, again and again and again. As soon as he feels me start to come, Jett goes over the edge too, slamming my hips down on his cock over and over, grinding my body against his. I feel his cock jerk; I can feel the long salty pulses of his cum as he empties himself inside me.

Marking me.

Jett slows for a few moments, then stops, breathing hard. His eyes are shut, which is a kind of relief. I don't want to stare into his eyes, no matter whether we just screwed or not. For a second we just stay like that, my forehead bowing to press again his.

Fuck. I have to move, otherwise his cum is going to drip out and go everywhere, I think.

I carefully disentangle myself, moving slowly. The last thing I want to do is hurt his piercing, so I'm extra careful. I sink onto my back, grabbing a pillow and wedging it underneath my hips.

"I'm trying to let gravity do its work," I explain when I see him giving me a questioning look.

"Sure," he shrugs. He turns over on his side, propping himself up with one hand. "I didn't hate any of that, by the way."

I chuckle, pulling a pillow over for my head. "That's good, because you're going to have to do it a lot to get me pregnant."

Milo makes his presence known, meowing quizzically. His little black tail is all I can see from my position, darting around the bed's frame. Jett sees him, putting his hand down and whistling, like Milo is a dog.

Unsurprisingly, Milo spurns Jett's attentions, meowing once more before darting out of the bedroom door.

Jett looks around my bedroom, his gaze landing on the only framed photo, sitting on my bedside table. He gets up, clearly comfortable with his naked body in a way that only hot guys are. Picking up the picture, he examines it.

I know the photo by heart. I am probably three years old, dark haired and clad in only a faded bathing suit. I'm sitting outside, on a dark-haired woman's lap. The woman is extremely thin, and she's looking at the camera with a steely kind of intensity. In the background, there is a tall man with a beard, but he's moving so the image is blurred.

"Is this your family?" he asks, his brow furrowing.

"Yes," I say, suddenly testy. "And that photo is the only one I have, so please put it back."

Jett raises a brow, but he puts it back. I can practically see the questions forming, written all over his handsome face. I don't want to answer them, though.

"Don't you have somewhere else to be?" I ask, keeping my tone neutral.

He looks mildly offended. "Are you kicking me out?"

I pull the bedspread across the bed and over my body so that I'm no longer naked.

"I'm just asking a question," I say.

His eyes narrow, but he just shrugs. "Sure."

He bends down to pick up his underwear, pulling them on. He finds his shirt and jeans and puts them on, his annoyance plain in his movements. Crap. I just wanted him to leave, I didn't actually mean to piss him off.

Silence echoes between us, amplifying every second as he gets ready to leave. He heads to the door of the bedroom, intending to leave on that note.

"Jett, wait," I say. I bite my lip.

He turns around impatiently. "What?"

"Thank you," I say, struggling to make words. "It was really nice. I… I like the way you fuck."

His expression is one of amusement and confusion.

"Uh… I like how you fuck too," he says, rubbing the back of his neck.

"Text me later?" I ask, hoping it's not too much to ask.

He sighs. "Yeah, okay."

Then he turns and leaves. A half minute later, I hear the door open and close.

"Fuuuuuuck!" I moan. I really could've handled that better, but I'm not sure how.

Whatever, I tell myself. It's better this way. Less a chance of you catching feelings.

I close my eyes and try to think of something else, anything else.

JETT

It's only been three days since she basically kicked me out of her apartment, but I can't stop thinking about Cady.

I find myself slipping into memories, remembering just how hot she was when she touched herself for me. Head thrown back, biting her luscious red lips, she enchanted me. And when she took my whole cock in her pussy for the first time?

Holy *fuck*.

My cock jumps to attention under my jeans as I'm sitting in standstill traffic. I glance at my phone, tempted to text her right this second. Then I think about how she was afterward, straight up asking me if I had somewhere to be.

It was so frosty that I needed a sweater. I wasn't expecting that kind of burn. She tried to make it up to me by asking me to text her later, but I got the message loud and clear.

I was just a tall, bearded, tattooed one-night stand type, who happened to be her sperm donor. Nothing more than that.

It is fine, really. But a part of me had sort of hoped that the two of us could at least be civil outside of our enthusiastic fucking.

The other part of me told that voice to shut the fuck up and take what was offered. Especially when what was offered involved such explosively good chemistry.

Just text her, I thought. Go and get some action, then dip out and still get a good night of sleep.

I stare at the cars ahead of me for a minute, then sigh and pick up my phone.

Hey. You working? I texted.

To my surprise, it's only a few seconds before she answers. *My place?*

She keeps it short, sweet, and to the point. I can't say that I blame her.

Yep. Be there whenever I get out of traffic. I-85 is a mess right now.

I'll be waiting.

I get to her place as soon as I can, and go through the whole rigamarole of buzzing at the door. When I get up to her door, just looking at the now-familiar slick black paint, the heavy gold number 16… it kinda turns me on.

I cock my head, considering that. She pulls the door open, and my heart skips a beat.

She answers the door wearing nothing but a set of wispy see-through red bra and panties. Her hair is pulled into a low braid, and she's wearing that same red lipstick. She grins at the dopey face that I'm making, stepping forward and grabbing me by the hand to pull me inside the apartment.

I close the door as she moves into the apartment, toward the bedroom.

She's right in front of me, and I can't resist the urge to reach out and grab her, to feel the silkiness of her lingerie under my fingertips. She turns in my arms, her dark hair and red lipstick so very vivid. Our lips meet, the kiss passionate and full of need.

I slide my hand to the back of her neck, a growl building in my throat. I feel the need to possess her, to own her, if just for this moment.

I deepen the kiss, realizing how much I needed this — I'd let it all build too long. Maybe that was why I was so fucking horny. She moans a little as she kisses me, coming up onto her toes to get closer.

Judging by her enthusiasm in returning the kiss, she felt the same.

I am desperate to feel Cady under my body. I feel like I'm going off the deep end a little, the urge to feel every single inch of her nearly overwhelming. I pick her up with one arm, carrying her backwards into the bedroom.

She was good the last time I had her, but this time there was something different about her. Intense, almost wild. She bit my bottom lip as I carried her back to the bed, and moaned.

"Please," she whispered as he put her down. "I need you to fuck me."

I reared back, looking down at her intently.

"You're just going to have to be patient, I guess."

I leaned down to kiss her lips, then moved to graze her ear, her neck. She shuddered with pleasure, her hands raking down my back. It reminded me that there was far too much material between us, my jeans and dark button-up shirt included.

I move back to peel my jacket off. Staring down at her with a distinctly threatening look, I close in again. She sat up close to the edge of the bed, and then we meet with a kiss, a clashing of lips and teeth.

I grip the back of her neck, force her to take more of

my kiss, to open her mouth more. She submits, but her eyes spark — she won't take it for long.

Good.

She undoes the buttons of my shirt. I close my eyes briefly as she kisses my stomach, her hands searching for my belt. I could see what she was doing, moving closer to getting me naked.

But I didn't want that, not just yet. I want to do all the things I skipped last time, the things I needed to try out with her. I caught her hands, tsking.

I release her and shuck my shirt. I take a few seconds to really fully appreciate the see through red bra and panties. I touch her nipple, which stands proudly alert. I teasing her by putting a couple of fingers inside the front of the panties.

"These are really fucking sexy," I say, looking up at her. "Now take them *off.*"

She is eager to comply, unhooking her bra and then slipping her panties down her incredible legs herself. I can't help but reach out and touch the curve of her hip, the swell of her breast. Her breasts are perfect, two gorgeous teardrops.

I push her back onto the bed, satisfied with her compliance. I quickly get undressed, leaving myself in dark boxer briefs. As soon as I move towards her, her hands are already on my boxers, pushing them down.

My cock bounces free, standing proudly. I look at Cady to see her reaction, and see something truly toe-curling: anticipation and hunger.

She doesn't back down for a second. She fists my cock in her hand boldly, making me hiss. I notice that she can't quite encircle it with her delicate fingers. As if I wasn't already hard enough, she gives my cock a few strokes.

Cady looks at me poignantly, then puts her red mouth

on the tip of my cock. I moan low in my throat. It's so wet and hot, and I have wondered so many times what her mouth would feel like. I keep wanting to close my eyes, but it's so erotic, watching her swirl the tip of my cock in her mouth.

I settle for watching and digging a hand into her low braid. I bite my lip as she repositions herself to take my cock deeper into her mouth.

She takes it deep, sucking it in long strokes. I nearly came on the first full one, and start reciting baseball stats in my head.

Jesus, she's fucking amazing.

She manages to wrap her hand most of the way around my cock, twisting as she worked her tongue gently under the head. I feel a strong need for control, a desire to dominate her.

Not yet, I think. Not today. But some day, I'm going to fuck her mouth.

Looking down on her as she works, watching her tongue move in and out... it nearly undoes me.

In less than five minutes, she has me ready to cum like an avalanche. I have to pull her away.

"That was amazing, but isn't the goal of this whole thing to get you pregnant?" I say, grinning.

She gives me a naughty glance while she wipes at her mouth. with the back of her hand. "Maybe."

I push her back onto the bed, all the way back to the pillows. I separate her thighs with a knee, then lay on top of her, kissing her hard.

She groans, ready for me. "Cum in me. You know you want to..."

I chuckled. As tempting as that sounds, there were important things to do first. Let it never be said that Cady walked away from this exchange without coming.

I move down, kissing my way across her breasts and her stomach as I go. She realizes what I am doing and tries to pull me back up to her lips, but I'm not standing for it.

I move down to the light dappling of hair she kept down there, spreading her lips wide with two fingers. She thrusts her hips and whimpers with hunger, impatient. She is soaked for me, beyond ready.

I delve in, running my tongue in circles, pulling soft sounds from her throat. Her hands clutch at my hair, breathless. I can tell how badly she wants it from just those sounds alone.

I keep my pace slow and steady. I listen to her breathing pick up, her hands restless. It's only when her hips began to move against my mouth, grinding mindlessly, that I kick up the intensity.

I pull back and insert one thick finger, then two before I put my tongue to work again. I work my fingers in and out, and put some force behind my tongue, working her clit for all it's worth.

"Please, Jett," she whimpers, writhing. "Please."

She is begging to cum now, pleading with me. I give her what she wants, using my tongue and my fingers to drive her over the edge.

She shatters, coming so hard around my fingers that I wince. She seems to come for ages, delicate aftershocks continuing for what seems like forever.

I move back up to her face, kissing her. She twines her fingers in my hair and presses against me, eager for more. I'm hard as a rock now, and she's about to experience everything I can give her.

I rise above her, fisting my cock, and rub the tip against her opening. She bites her lip and pulls at me, gasping at the way that I fill her. I groan a little as I sink down. Her pussy is so incredible, it feels like a glove made just for me.

"You like that, don't you?" I say, as I start to move.

"Yes," she cried. "God, Jett, fuck me harder."

I managed to reign myself in, filling her with short strokes, keeping things on the lighter side.

Well, the lighter side for me, anyway.

I could feel her nails raking my back; I feel the pressure building, pressure to just let go, let the beast out of its cage.

No, not yet...

I fuck her in measured increments, even as I realize that I won't last that long like this. I need her to take some of the control, to take some of the burden, or I am going to fucking come everywhere. I'm not ready for that yet, and she doesn't seem ready either.

I slow, kissing her, then pull out. I flip us both, reversing our positions.

"Your turn," I tell her, breathless. "Show me what you got."

Cady gave me a slow grin, mounting me like a horse. Again, I felt that slippery-tight fit, like she was created for me. She is beautiful in this position, breasts jutting out, bouncing as she begins to move. I take full advantage, running my hands down her neck and cupping her breasts.

It feels so good, in such a different way. Watching her move is truly something else.

Her face when she starts to ride me... I can't look anywhere else. It is transfixing, the way she wears her emotions on her sleeve like that. She lifts her face toward the sky as she gets closer; I could feel her tightening like a spring.

"Are you close?" I whisper, already knowing the answer.

I reach up and caress her breast, pinch her nipples.

"Yes. More!" she says, holding my hand to her breast.

Her hips moved fast, her eyes are closed tight. I

love the way I can feel the tightening of her core around my cock. I can tell she wants it, but the part of my brain that longs for control just can't let her have it.

Not yet, not if I'm not giving it to her.

When I lift her up, she protests, her eyes snapping open. "Hey!"

"On your knees," I say, roughly putting her in the right position. "Let me see you touch yourself."

She reaches a trembling hand down to do as I say. I watch for a moment as she touches herself, softly gasping as she works over her clit. It's hotter than anything I've ever seen, and I've seen a lot.

I grasp my cock, fit it against her pussy, and plunge in. We both cry out as I slide home, filling her to the hilt.

"Your pussy feels so good," he whispers. "So wet, so tight. God, you're fucking perfect."

Now the beast can come out of its cage, I decide. I unleash it upon both of us. I hammer her from behind, gritting my teeth.

I can feel her tightening again, ready to orgasm. I set a grueling pace, my mind narrowly focused on one thing: the orgasm barreling down on me.

I feel her beginning to come underneath me with a scream. I completely let myself go. My movements are brutal, unforgiving.

I come with a shout, pumping long jets of my semen into her willing body. We both slump forward, and I manage to move a little so that she's not completely underneath my body. I can't talk or even breathe for a minute afterward.

I run two fingertips down her sweat-dampened spine, just to see her shiver. I like how responsive her whole body is, how easy it is to make her do or feel however I want.

Our legs are still tangled together, and I trail my hand down to caress her hip, her thigh.

I'm still turned on, apparently, because my cock stirs against her skin. She looks at me, halfway between impressed and about to roll her eyes.

"Really?" she says.

"Hey, it's not my body's fault that your body looks like this," I shrug. I knead her ass cheek a little, playful.

She shifts and I move, letting her roll over. I smile at the sheer disarray that is happening to her hair; I get a little kick that I made it a fucking mess. I reach out to tuck a tendril behind her ear, then lighten things up by cupping the fullness of one of her bare breasts.

"Do you maybe want to get dinner tomorrow?" I ask. The words are out of my mouth before I've even thought about them.

Immediately, I can see that she's skeptical. She thinks it's a terrible idea.

"Dinner?" she asks, scrunching her face. "Umm... doesn't that seem kind of... against the grain, for us? I mean, I wouldn't want any wires getting crossed or lines blurred, you know?"

"Right," I say, shaking my head. I feel the beginning of a little color in my cheeks. "I meant as friends. You know, just... to get to know each other more. The more that we trust each other..."

I trail off, but she doesn't pick up my hint. Instead, she grows teasing. "The more we can... what? Braid each others' hair?"

"I meant that the more we get to know each other, the kinkier we can get," I say. I sit up, looking around for my underwear. I swear, this is becoming too familiar a pattern.

"Oh," Cady says, thoughtful. "I hadn't really considered that."

"It doesn't matter," I say, keeping my tone neutral. I find my shirt and my jeans, pulling them on. "I should go. I have a big day tomorrow, and I want to hit the gym before work."

"Umm, alright," she says. "You know how to reach me."

I grab my boots and give her a half wave as I leave. I almost kiss her goodbye, then decide against it.

You're just a piece of ass, I think. You know how this goes.

Still doesn't keep me from being in a terrible mood as I leave her apartment, though.

CADY

I'm coming over now.

That is all the warning I received, about five minutes before Jett showed up at my doorstep. I put down the pen I was using to correct a brief, a tiny bit surprised. After he left last time, after I shot down his idea of going out, I was worried that he would take it wrong.

It just seemed to me that getting involved as more than fuck buddies is… well, problematic. Because I can't look at him and not go all googly-eyed inside, not when he gives me that lopsided smile of his.

And as I have previously reminded myself, he is not boyfriend material. Besides, I don't even want a man.

…right?

No, I don't, I tell myself.

He startles me from my thoughts by buzzing the door downstairs. *Shit!*

I rush to the door, casting a disapproving eye at my clothes; he didn't even give me time to change out of my yoga pants and t-shirt.

I open the door and eye him, looking good as ever in a

blue plaid button up and blue jeans. I swear, that blue plaid is just the color of his eyes.

I blush when I realize that I'm already getting wet.

He does this to me.

"Like what you see, princess?" he growls.

He steps in, closing the door and sweeping me off my feet. He carries me to the bedroom, taking my hair down for me.

"I like it down," he says, twining a length around his finger. "I like to feel it around me, to see it grow as wild as you do."

Jett reaches a hand down to my face, brushing my hair from my eyes. He tucks it gently behind my ear, fixating me with his piercingly blue eyes.

"It's okay. I like you looking at me. I like *seeing* you looking at me more."

"Even then, it's rude to stare." I avert my gaze and focus on my knee instead.

"Princess, you can stare at me all you want. As long as it's me you're staring at like that, I'm happy. Fucking ecstatic, actually." He cups my chin so that our eyes meet. He holds my gaze, still not moving to hide any part of himself.

I start tracing the lines of the tattoos on his chest, then the ones on his arm, all the way to his hand. Next, I trace the muscular lines of his stomach down to his hips.

His breath hitches, and his cock twitches. I bit my lip, and he lets out a low moan.

"I'm really trying to let you do your thing here, princess. But you're really fucking killing me."

I grin at his words. A shiver of excitement runs up my spine and I can feel myself growing wet already.

"Fuck," he breathes as I run my hands over the outline of his hard cock over his briefs. "I can't fucking wait to get inside of you."

He flips me onto my back and presses his body to mine, kissing me deeply. He traces the neckline of my tank top as he ran his other hand up and down my thigh.

I moan as he reaches for the hem of my shirt, but I am surprised; instead of my shirt, he starts pulling off my yoga pants. I help him, and the second he has got them off, he's like a kid in a candy store.

He runs his hands up and down my smooth legs, looking at them like they are something delicious to be eaten. The look makes the fine hair on my neck rise. I'm glad that I know, because if a stranger looked at me with that kind of naked lust in his eyes, I would be afraid.

With Jett, though, fear is impossible. Not when he looks at me, or when he kisses me. I close my eyes for a second, nearly overcome.

"Cady," he says softly. "Look into my eyes for a second." I open my eyes and he drinks me in. He spends a minute running one hand up and down my side, leaving goosebumps in his trail. He teases my nipples through my shirt, planting soft kisses on the exposed skin on my stomach.

I barely manage a nod. My skin is on fire everywhere he touches me, aching for more. Each stroke on my nipples causes my pussy to clench.

I am pretty sure that by now, my panties are drenched. I would be embarrassed, if I could bring myself to think that far. But all my thoughts are completely focused on what he is making me feel.

His hands slide my panties down, and my tank top disappears over my head. If this were anyone else, I would be trying to cover up, but I force myself not to. The way he was looking at my body, his eyes dark with lust, make me feel hot and naughty.

He does this to me.

He drinks me in with his eyes, growling softly as his fingers stroke my dripping slit.

"God, Cady. You're so fucking wet."

He brings his glistening fingers to his lips, licking my juices off the tips of his fingers. He closes his eyes and lets out a low moan as he tastes me on his hands. "Fucking delicious, princess. So sweet. I can't fucking wait to taste more."

I focused on his fingers, that are once more playing with my clit, teasing the seam of my pussy.

He kisses me deeply, hungrily. I could feel his rock hard cock digging into my soft belly. I moan loudly, still unable to form any words.

"Fuck, Cady. I've never cum from just sounds before, but if you keep that up, that might change." His voice was husky, low.

"Yes, please Jett! Please!" I beg.

I barely register that I haven't showered yet, before his mouth is licking slowly but hungrily along my seam. Up and down, sucking in my lips, darting his tongue into me before starting all over again. He lets out a low moan again.

"So fucking sweet, Cady." He moans before taking my sensitive clit in his mouth, sucking lightly, his tongue flicking against my bud.

It's a little like being struck by lightning, that first touch of his tongue to my clit. His tongue is turning me into a shivering, moaning maniac.

I try to buck my hips against him, unable to contain myself any longer, but his strong hands on my hips kept me in place. He licks and sucks until I see nothing but stars and fireworks, feeling like I am about to fly away if it wasn't for him anchoring me.

Far too soon, the pressure that had been building up

inside me releases into a ball of light. My mind shatters in every different direction possible as I scream his name, digging my fingers into his shoulders and tugging at his hair.

He keeps licking, although he is very gentle now, aware of how sensitive I must be. I have to pull him away, and he comes up looking immensely self-impressed.

"Not bad, huh?" he says, licking at his mouth.

"Not bad indeed." I tug him close for a kiss and taste my own juices, sharp and sweet.

He pushes his boxer briefs off and moves to lay between my legs. I can feel the blunt tip of his cock against my entrance, positioned perfectly to slide into my pussy. He doesn't though.

He just kisses me hard. I can still taste myself on his lips. Somehow, it just arouses me even more. I moan into his mouth, and hear a low sound at the back of his throat.

"You want it?" he says, so low it's almost a whisper.

"You fucking know I do."

He moves a little, shifts very slightly, and I can feel the promise of his weight, his body heat. I shiver.

"Are you sure?" he asks, teasing now.

"I want you inside of me. Now! Please, Jett."

He lets out a low growl, but doesn't say any more. I can feel his hard cock gently pushing harder at my entrance. He slides in slowly, watching my every facial expression, seemingly gauging my every move.

"Fuck, so tight," he breathes as he stretches me inch by inch.

Pleasure fills my body, taking over every inch of me. The entire world disappears. All that exists is the feeling of his cock in me, his body on mine, breathing deeply and softly growling and moaning into my ears. He kisses me and whispers to me.

"Fuck, you're so good, Cady."

He rocks into me with perfect rhythm, with just the right amount of pressure. I can feel my body begin to tighten, to draw taut like a bowstring.

It is so good, yet almost painful at this point. I feel so delightfully used, feel stretched out by his massive cock. I know he isn't going to stop, but that doesn't keep me from encouraging him.

"Don't stop, Jett. I'm so close," I urge. "I'm right there. Make me come."

I know he can. I will him to release the tension building in my breasts, in my core. His breathing is ragged now. I can feel his muscles starting to shake as he thrust into me more forcefully, but he was still taking care not to hurt me. He was nearly there, and I am right there with him.

A final thrust and my world shatters into a million pieces again. The knot that had been building inside me releases.

He nips at my bottom lip, then his eyes roll back, his muscular shoulders flexing, his thighs shaking as he fills me to the brim. I feel his orgasm pour into my core, his cock twitching deep inside of me.

And it is the most exquisite thing.

As we're lying there, breathing hard, Jett surprises me. He rolls over, self-assured as ever, and starts talking.

"I was thinking about that first night. You know, when we were supposed to bang, but I wouldn't have sex with you?" he asked, drawing a figure eight on the bedspread. "I judged you for drinking, but I shouldn't have. I don't expect you to sit around, waiting for me and my magic dick."

I raise my eyebrows, surprised. "Thanks, but you don't have to apologize. You ate my pussy like it was your job. I'm not mad about it."

I don't know how much I like knowing that I was judged for it and found wanting... but there is something very honest and refreshing about his admission.

He is quiet for a few seconds, his eyes cast downward as he studies whatever invisible design he's drawing on my bed. I give him time to think, busying myself with inspecting his tattoos. His tattoos seem to start in the center of his muscular chest, where a family crest takes up a good bit of space, lions and swords in bold yellow and blue ink.

Around that, there is a border of roses... and then from there his tattoos are more erratic. I spy a tiger on his shoulder, a flaming heart on his bicep, and a satanic-looking cherub at the top of his ribs.

I catch his hand, reading the words tattooed on his knuckles. "Hold... let me see your other hand? Ahhh, hold fast."

"Mhmm," he says. "I always felt like I needed something to hold onto when I was a kid. My uh... my dad drank a lot, and it kind of made our house... chaotic."

I look up at him, taken aback for the second time in a handful of minutes. "Is that why you didn't want me to be drunk?"

Jett lifts a shoulder, shrugging. He doesn't say anything for a second. When he does, it's not at all what I expect.

"Don't worry about alcoholism being passed down through my genes," he says, his dark blue eyes pinning me. "When I grew up, I figured out that he's not my biological dad."

Whoa. This is pretty heavy stuff for pillow talk.

I open my mouth to say something, but he waves it away.

"That's a little personal for the moment. Forget I said anything," he says. He sits up and looks around for his boxer briefs.

"It's fine. I was going to ask—"

He cuts me off. "If I know who my biological father is, so you can ask me questions about his health?"

I make a face. He doesn't know me that well. I need to put him in his place.

"Uh, *no*. I was going to ask if you want me to order a pizza. I'm starving. Oooh or something with chocolate. I love chocolate."

Jett shakes his head. "Nah, I should get going. Thanks, though."

I roll onto my side and watch him as he gets dressed. I admire his body as he bends and flexes. He is so confident and self-assured; I'm definitely jealous of that.

"You sure about the pizza?" I ask.

Jett looks at me out of the corner of his eye, and then shakes his head.

"Do I want to do something that involves hiding out here some more? Not really."

Just what is that supposed to mean? I make a curious face, but he doesn't bite.

"I'll see you later, okay?" he says. He's already halfway out the door, so I don't bother to answer.

I do wonder what is going on in his mind, though. I think about what he said, about *hiding out here some more*. Does that mean if I had asked if he wanted to go grab something to eat outside the house, that would've been fine?

That's crazy, though. He's not the one I'm worried about. I'm setting the boundaries up like they are so that I don't fall for *him*. I make an aggravated *grrrr* sound, because men are forever trampling all over the boundaries we women set for them.

I settle back for a minute, then grab my phone and call Olive.

"Pizza?" I ask in lieu of a greeting.

"That's all you had to say! I'll be over soon," she says, hanging up.

At least she *wants to have pizza with me*, I think. I always have my friendship with Olive, even if I don't have any reliable male companionship.

Men suck anyway, I huff.

Getting up, I head to my closet to put something on.

JETT

I'm already out with Alex and Mason, appreciating some beer at the Orpheus brewery, when Cady texts me.

Hey. What are you doing?

I read the message while Mason is telling us about the marathon he just ran. I'm only half paying attention to him, checking my phone under the massive oak table, but I give myself away when I try to think of how to respond.

"Hey, rock star," Mason says. "Eyes up here."

"Or just tell us what's on the phone," Alex chips in. "If he has a line with some girls, he'd better cough it up."

I roll my eyes. I haven't told Alex and Mason that I've been seeing Cady yet, but I guess now is as good a time as any.

"Remember that girl from the party a few weeks ago? The one you dared me to... I don't know, not take home?" I say to Mason.

He straightens a little. "The hottie who you said wasn't your type? Yeah, I remember."

"Well, she and I have been—"

"Boning?" Mason cuts in.

"Yeah, if that's what you want to call it, you fucking little kid."

Mason grins, unabashed. "It is!"

"Well, she's texting me." I pull my phone up from under the table. "I'm just going to tell her I'll call her later."

"Wait, whoa whoa," Alex interjects, putting his hand over my phone screen. "I think you should ask her if she has any hot friends who like beer. There's plenty of room here at our table."

I start to say no, but Mason cuts me off again. "I second that motion. Bring the girls here, to me."

He jabs a finger into the table. I squint at him; he might be a little drunk.

"What's the girl's name?" Alex asks, brow furrowing.

"Uhhh it's Cady," I say. "And... I don't know, aren't we sort of having a bro date?"

"Fuck no," Mason says immediately. "Not if there can be women."

I think about it, cupping my jaw. The last time I was with her, I did sort of make a big deal out of the fact that we never leave her house. Her answer to an invitation *could* answer whether or not I'm crazy to even be thinking about dating her.

"Alright, fine. I'll ask," I relent.

"Atta boy," Mason says, clapping me on the back super hard.

I make a face as I reply to her. I settle on: *Out with my friends at a brewery. All guys, no girls. Do you have any friends to fill our party out?*

I see that she's gotten the text. Those three dots appear, letting me know that she's typing. Then they disappear.

I flip my phone over on the table, shaking my head. "She's not answering."

As soon as the words are out of my mouth, my phone buzzes in my hands. Alex raises his brows.

"Guess you're not the patient type?" he jokes.

My friend Olive is down for some day drinking. Where are you guys?

I text back with the details, and she says they're on their way.

"She's bringing one friend, someone named Olive?" I say, uncertain about the whole idea.

"You know what you need?" Mason asks.

"Another beer?"

"Another beer, exactly." He gets up and grabs our pitcher, heading out of the tiny room with the bar in mind.

It doesn't take long for Cady and her friend to get here. I see Cady come into our room, and it's like she's moving in slow motion: her dark hair is in a messy side braid, her grey eyes are sparkling, and she is wearing a blood red dress that is short enough to make me shift in my seat. She sees me, which makes her give me a megawatt smile.

Fuck. Between her miles of bare, toned legs and that red-lipped smile, I'm on the verge of getting hard, right here and now.

Her friend Olive is just behind her, a petite redhead in a pastel blue floral dress. Alex and Mason both sit up a little straighter when they notice the girls; I realize dumbly, for the first time, that I'm not the only one who finds Cady attractive.

"Hey stranger," Cady says, stopping before the table. "Mind if we join you?"

"Hey," I say, rising to greet her. I awkwardly kiss her on the cheek and hug her. Her dress is really tantalizingly short. I nearly brush her amazing bare legs when I stoop to hug her. Almost. "Here, sit down. This is Mason, and this big guy is Alex."

The girls take empty seats for themselves, slinging their purses across the chairs as a way of claiming them. Cady sits next to me, and I scoot my seat a little closer to hers. Mason starts fumbling with the spare pint glasses that we brought back from the bar, and filling them with the amber lager that we decided to try.

"This is my best friend Olive," Cady says, putting her hand on Olive's back. "She was with me at Ponce Market, getting some flowers, and she agreed to come along."

"Yes I did," says Olive. "Mmmm."

I want to laugh at the look on Olive's face. It's like she's at the meat market, and she's trying to pick the best rack of ribs. That makes me, Mason, and Alex slabs of meat, which I think is an apt comparison. It's not often that we are the objectified ones, I guess.

Mason slides Cady and Olive each a glass. I scrunch my face a bit as Olive's glass stops abruptly and sloshes a little over the rim. "Thanks," the girls say in unison.

Cady takes a sip of the beer, eyeballing the pint glass. "Hmmm. I thought it would be more bitter."

Alex shakes his head. "No, not this particular beer. It's very low in hops, so it has a correspondingly lower bitterness."

"Alex brews at home," I tell them. "He is a beer snob, big time. It was hard to get him to agree to drink this amber lager, actually."

"I like what I like," he says with a shrug. "Hey, at least I'm not like Mr. Whiskey Aficionado over here."

He jerks his thumb at Mason. Mason looks fake-offended.

"It's not my fault that you guys like fucking Bulleit. I happen to have a refined palate—"

"Alright, alright," I interrupt. "Let's not get into that again. Cady, I know you're a lawyer. Olive, what do you do?"

"Well, she's the lawyer you want when you're trying to sue Big Pharma," Olive says, pointing to Cady. "Me? I'm the lawyer you want when you've done something very, very bad, but you don't want to go to jail for it."

Cady gives Olive a funny look. "Or if you're innocent, I would assume."

Olive snorts. "They so rarely are, though. Honestly, I think I'm a very important part of the legal system. It is your right to defend yourself, no matter what."

"And if you happen to have a mere five hundred thousand dollars, you too can have Olive on your team," Cady jokes.

"Hey, nobody said the law was cheap," Olive answers, looking at her nails.

"No, indeed. So what do you guys do? Aside from Jett. Obviously I already know what he does," Cady says.

"My boy Mason here is a grade-A, genuine bounty hunter," I jump in. "And Alex is in the NFL, although he's a free agent right now."

Olive looks confused. "He's what?"

Alex speaks up. "Um, it means I'm not signed to a team at the moment."

"Ahh," Olive says, and Cady nods her understanding. "So are you like... looking for one? Or how does that work?"

I lean back in my seat, letting the conversation flow around me. Cady looks at me after a second, and I wink at her. She blushes. I stretch out, putting my arm around her. I draw lazy circles on her silk-clad shoulder, which makes her blush even harder.

Yeah, I'll admit it. This is exactly what I hoped for, us going out with our friends and her acting like a...

Well, shit. She's acting like a girlfriend. Not like Emily, obviously; Emily was frosty from the get-go, and she never liked my friends.

Cady moves her chair a little closer to mine, so that we're practically touching. I tug her side braid gently, and she looks at me with a grin. I want to lean in and whisper something dirty in her ear, but that would probably be rude to everyone else.

So I just think about what I want to do to her, and how. I will rip that little red dress off of her... or no, maybe I will let her leave it on, while I fuck her senseless. In my mind, I do her doggystyle, pound her as her fantastic ass jiggles.

Fuck, I'm hard again.

I'm so distracted by the thought of what I'd like to do with her, I almost don't notice when her hand touches my knee. I glance at her, and see that she's purposely looking away. After looking around, I feel fairly confident that my lower half is covered by the table.

When her hand moves further and further up my thigh, so close to touching my cock, it's very hard to maintain a neutral expression. I put my hand under the table and grab her hand, dragging it to my cock. I see her eyes go wide, and I love the blush that springs to her cheeks.

Before she can start to explore, though, I remove both of our hands, placing them on her silky thigh. She glances at me with a tight smirk, her eyes sparkling. She's flirting with me, big time.

I like her. Like... I really like her. And she gets along fine with my friends, unlike my ex.

The thoughts come to me, unasked for. But there they are. I give her thigh a hard squeeze, enjoying the feel of my fingers on her smooth skin. She gives me another smirk, and then answers a question that Mason asked.

There's only one problem with my liking her. She was pretty damned explicit about what she's looking for in a guy: great genes, a good time… and absolutely no commitment. I'm not sure how far I should take the whole no commitment thing, but I'm pretty sure that telling her out loud that I like her is a no-no.

I give her a gentle squeeze, then release her.

"Hey, how about a group selfie?" Olive suggests, whipping her phone out.

"Uhhh…" Mason says, looking at me for help.

"Pleeeeeeeease," Olive says.

"She likes to print them out and put them onto a big wall of photos at her house. It kind of makes her look like a creepy murderer," Cady says.

I shrug. "Why not?"

Mason groans, but the rest of us submit to Olive's picture-taking. I smile and casually put my arm around Cady's shoulders. When there's no resistance, I'm a little surprised.

After four selfies, Mason shakes his head. "We're done."

I detach myself from Cady. I look around at everyone's glasses, and the empty pitcher. "Should I get another round?"

"Yes! Oooh, do they have anything fruity?" Olive asks.

"If you get a fruit beer, we can't be friends anymore," Alex says coolly.

"You could get both," Mason suggests. "We're reasonable people, after all."

I chuckle. "All right. Something with fruit, and something without."

"Extra hoppy!" Alex insists.

"Alright, alright, don't get carried away. I'll be back." I stand up and grab the pitcher.

"I'll keep you company," Cady says, jumping up. "Make sure you don't get lost on the way back."

I grin, offering her my hand. After a moment of hesitation, she slips her hand into mine. I give her hand a squeeze as I head out of the back room. There is a line at the bar, and we stand and wait our turn.

"Your hand is so much smaller than mine," I say, looking down at our clasped hands. "Here, let's compare sizes."

I hold my hand up. She brushes back a strand of her hair, and holds her hand up against mine. There is almost an inch of difference between the tops of her fingers and the tops of mine.

"That explains some things about you," she says, her eyes twinkling.

"Are you trying to say that I have a big cock?" I ask, loud enough for the guy in front of us to turn around for a second.

Her cheeks color that perfect dusty rose tinge. She drops her voice to a whisper. "Maybe."

I bite my lip, leaning close enough to her that my lips touch her ear. She shudders before I even say anything.

"I'm going to take you from behind later… and it's not going to be sweet. It's going to be rough. I'm going to spread you out and dominate you," I rasp into her ear. I put my hand on her waist, then slip it around to her back. "You're going to fucking love it."

Cady's eyes are so wide when I look at her, her pupils dilated. Instead of saying anything, she grabs my bearded face and kisses me, hard. I can feel her need in that kiss, and that is more meaningful than anything else.

"Hey, you guys are next," the lady behind me points out, impatient.

"Sorry," Cady murmurs.

I wink at her and move up to the bar. But the gears in my head are turning, trying to figure out my next move.

CADY

It was almost midnight by the time that Jett finally came, shouting my name. We both collapsed where we were, me on top of him, both of us breathing hard. I like this position that we're in; it lets me feel all the raw power of the man below me.

Right now he's as relaxed as likely he ever will be, but I can still feel his abs and pecs… and probably a thousand other muscles for which I don't know the name. I turn my face to lay it flat against his muscular, sweat-slicked chest.

I can hear the insistent tha-thump tha-thump tha-thump of his heart, and the sound of him inhaling and exhaling. It's so rhythmic and lulling, it makes my eyelids heavy. I want to close my eyes and fall asleep as I listen to it.

Lazily, I wonder what kind of gym routine he does to keep in shape. His arms are each almost as big around as one of my legs. And thank god he does all that, because it results in some mind blowing sex.

"Jesus christ," he mumbles, moving some of my hair so it's not in his face. "That was fucking spectacular."

I just grunt, which makes him chuckle. I like the sound of it, with my ear pressed to his chest. It's just very... him. He puts his arms under his head and sighs contently.

I wiggle a little bit, and catch sight of my family photograph. I was so rude to him when he asked about it; I feel embarrassed, retroactively.

"Hey," I say after a minute.

"Yeah?" he asks. The rumble I can feel when he talks is so fucking nice.

"You know the photo of me and my family?"

He pauses for several beats. "Yeah..."

"It's... my mom is holding me," I say slowly. "And I think the guy in the background is my dad, but I don't really know for sure."

He takes a second to digest that. "How did you come across the picture? You said you were raised in an orphanage, right?"

"Sort of. Mostly foster care homes. I, uh..." I pause, drawing a breath. "Sorry, it's really hard for me to talk about... about my family."

He shifts a bit, one of his hands coming down to stroke my bare back. For some reason, that gives me the courage to keep talking.

"So, I was taken away by the state at seven, I think. Well, from what I can piece together. I requested my case files as an adult, and it said that... well, basically my mom was brutally beaten by a man. Maybe the guy was my father, maybe not. And it wasn't the first time he hit her, either. They pulled me because he had beaten me too, and my mom wouldn't leave him. I think..."

I feel tears burning at the corner of my eyes. I hate crying.

But I can't stop seeing the scene in my head, what little I remember. My mom was in a pink shirt and white panties, and the man was in blue jeans and a yellow cutoff shirt. I saw the man leaning over my mom, staring down at her as she crouched on the floor by the cabinets. She was already protecting herself, drawing up into a little ball as he yelled at her.

I hear the words he said, still drilled into me to this day. *You fucking whore! I saw you flirting with the neighbor, bitch. You think that any man would want you now, all fucking fat and pregnant? No! I don't think so.*

I take a minute to breathe, to ensure that I wasn't about to make a scene. I calm down, get him out of my head. Still, I get goosebumps when I think about it. I have a real and complex fear of getting pregnant and then being dependent on anyone else for my well-being.

Jett seems content to just lie there, stroking my back. He seems to have nothing to say about my little lapse, and that's okay by me.

"Sorry," I say at last.

"Don't apologize to me," he says. "You're just being honest."

"Anyway, my mom gave me a few things to keep. And that photo is one of them."

Silence stretches between us. I can tell he has a question, but isn't sure how to ask it. I glance up at him.

"You want to know something, I can tell," I say.

"I was just going to ask… what happened to her? Your mom, I mean."

I purse my lips. I really, really don't like talking about this, but I did open the door.

"The guy that she wouldn't leave killed her," I bite out. "And he ran. The police barely looked for him, just figured… you know… she was asking for it."

Jett looked horrified. "Jesus, Cady. I'm so sorry."

I look away, using my fingertips to dash tears from my

eyes. He rubs my back, up and down my spine. It feels so good, so comforting, that I want to let my tears run free. I almost tell him to stop, but then I would have to explain what's going on inside my head.

Instead, I change the subject. "I feel like… I have a chance to do a better job with my own family, you know? Like it's a second chance or something. I think that's why I'm so baby crazy."

He just nodded. "That makes sense."

"Ahhh," I say, wiping my tears away. Milo meows, and jumps up onto my side on the bed. I shift a bit so that I can pet him, even though it's pretty awkward. "Enough of that. Tell me about something else. Tell me about your family."

"Oh…" Jett says. He tries to pet Milo by reaching over my body, but Milo ducks. "Umm. It's just me and my brother now. Jax."

"Are you close? And is this an older brother, or a younger one?" I ask, not moving from my position on his chest. I keep listening to the rise and fall of his chest as he breathes.

"Younger. And we're not really that close. You know, I didn't grow up in a very good home either. Although nothing like yours, I'm sure."

I lift my head to gaze at him. His eyes are downcast, like he has something to be ashamed of, but I'm sure that isn't true.

"You said your mom used to drink?" I prompt him gently.

"Yeah." He nods slowly. "Actually, my mom drank *and* did a lot of drugs. Me and Jax were always the kids who showed up to school with holes in our shoes, wearing clothes that were the wrong sizes and hadn't seen a wash in a while. We just…"

He pauses for a breath. "You know how your mom is

supposed to be the one person that cares about you more than anything else? Like, you always hear about moms going above and beyond for their kids? My mom wasn't like that. My mom was broken. Me and Jax came after a lot of other stuff on her priority list."

My heart breaks for him, in that moment. I know *exactly* how he feels. I swear that I see a tear glistening in his dark blue eye before he blinks it away.

"I am so sorry," I say, running my hand across his shoulder, starting to stroke him.

"I mean, it's fine," he says, resuming rubbing my back.

"No, it' not fine. It sounds like you had a really shitty upbringing."

"Yeah, but at least CPS never took us away." He shrugs. "You still win."

I can't help the giggle that emerges from my chest. Jett glances down at me, and I put my hand over my mouth. My laughter apparently upsets Milo, who jumps off the bed and vanishes.

"Sorry. I just… the idea of winning struck me as funny. Who had the worse childhood, the orphan or the alcoholic's kid?" I say.

"I'm glad I could provide some levity to the situation," he rumbles.

"Hey, it's not my fault. I just have a morbid sense of humor."

"Hah hah," he says, enunciating each syllable. Jett shifts me a little, and I slide off of him. I brace my head with a hand, and he rolls onto his side to mirror me.

"You want to hear something totally, completely fucked up?" he asks. "I'm only telling you because I think you might be able to relate."

"Tell me! I promise not to judge."

"When I was a kid, I used to lie awake at night. You

know, I shared the pull out couch with Jax. And he was always a sound sleeper, he would be out the second his head hit the pillow. I was always so envious of that. Anyway, I used to lie awake and listen to whatever was going on in my mom's bedroom. Her arguing with whoever her boyfriend was that week. Or sometimes they would fuck; I pulled my pillow over my head during that."

He pauses, then continues. "I used to lie there, with my pillow over my head, and wish that something would happen to my mom. Like, she would get into a car wreck, or die some other common death. And then… in my mind… Jax and I would make it on our own, like the kid from Home Alone."

His expression is so guilty, I reach out and slip my arms around him, hugging him tightly.

"You were a kid," I say simply. "You didn't make it happen."

"Nah. My mom died of liver failure a few years ago. It would have been a blessing if she'd died in a car crash, honestly. Instead, me and Jax and my aunt were huddled around her hospital bed, watching her tweak out on painkillers. It didn't seem… pleasant."

I didn't know what to say to that, so I just hugged him again. "I'm sorry."

"It's okay," he says again, brushing it all under the rug. "Actually, it's getting pretty late…"

I bite my lip. "You know, you can stay over if you want. Since it's so late."

Jett looks at me, his expression unreadable. Then he slowly shakes his head. He disentangles himself from me and starts looking for his clothes.

"I have to get up early," he says. "It'll be easier if I'm at my own place."

He pulls on his pants and then buttons up his shirt.

"What's your schedule like this week?" I ask, brushing back a lock of my hair.

"Pretty relaxed. You?"

"Relaxed is not a word in my vocabulary, when it comes to work. I'll be around later at night, though."

He stuffs his feet in his shoes and smiles. "Alright. Sounds good."

He heads out. The front door opens and closes, and Jett is gone. I lie back, thinking about what I learned tonight.

Jett is pretty badly damaged, just like me. Like me, you would never guess it from the way he acts. You have to be a part of his inner circle, I guess.

Does that mean I'm part of his inner circle? Maybe.

It also makes sense that I'm so attracted to him. An old therapist said that chemistry is just sensing compatible damage on another person. I think that is right, in light of what I just learned.

I start wondering about Jett, about what it is that he wants from this… well, relationship, I guess.

I want a baby, which I've been crystal clear about.

But what does he want? Does he even know?

I roll onto my stomach, sighing.

JETT

"Two of the salmon filets, please?" I say to the white-outfitted guy behind the meat counter at Whole Foods. He points to two, and I nod. "Yeah, those are perfect."

I'm planning on cooking dinner for Cady, because I have yet to see her eat anything that didn't come in a plastic to-go bag. Also, she's never been to my place. For some reason, I have a feeling that she will be skittish about it.

Thus, I have something to offer, aside from the promise of more sex. Salmon and asparagus and maybe some bread. That sounds pretty good.

And I'll have her for dessert, my man-brain interjects.

The guy hands me the paper-wrapped salmon, and I head to the bakery section. I pick out a loaf of bread, then wander up to the register. A few minutes later, I'm out the door with my purchases, heading for my car.

I pop the passenger door open and deposit my groceries, then close the door. When I do, I nearly run headlong into Emily. A petite blonde nymph, Emily's whole face scrunches when she sees that I'm the one who nearly ran into her.

"Jett?" she says, sounding puzzled. As if this Whole Foods isn't a place I shop for food or something. It's actually the only place that I ever shopped the whole time that we were together, because it's around the corner from my house.

"Hey," I say, unsure how this will go. "It's... been a while."

"Yeah, it has," she says, juggling a grocery bag. She's wearing a yoga outfit, a white tank top and black stretchy pants, so I figure that's where she just came from. "You look really good."

"Uh... thanks," I say, feeling awkward as fuck. "Umm, you too. You do yoga around here?"

"What?" she says, then looks down at her outfit. "Oh, yeah. My friend just opened a pilates studio right across the way. So... I'll be around this way a lot more again."

She says again because she practically lived with me during the last year we were together. I was hesitant about having her move in every time that we talked about it. I just... I don't know. I didn't want her to inhabit *my* space, I guess. It was pretty selfish.

"Right," I say. I look at my watch, because I'm trying to time my texts to Cady with when she's getting off of work.

"Listen, the CrossFit gym that I'm a member at has a 5k fun run coming up in a couple of weeks," she says, juggling the bag of groceries again. "Do you maybe... want to run it with me?"

I dumbstruck for a second. "I... what... a fun run?"

I sound like a complete an utter idiot, repeating her words back to her.

Emily flashes me a grin. "Yeah, you know. Assuming that you haven't gotten serious with anyone, of course."

Cady's face flashes in my mind. Would I call that serious, though?

Cady probably wouldn't.

"No," I say, though I already feel like a liar. "No one serious."

"Cool," she says, pushing back her blonde hair. "It's on the seventeenth, if you're really interested. I think there is an after-party at Fado when it's over, too. I know you like a good Irish stout after a workout."

She winks. She's right, of course. I do like a heavy beer after a hard workout.

The real question is whether or not Emily is really asking me out. I mean, she's got to be, right? That's the only reason she'd ask me to run this race with her.

"Right," I say, jiggling my key fob. "I'll see if my schedule is free."

"Great!" she says. She looks down a little. "I've missed you a lot since... you know."

Since you ripped my heart out and stomped on it? I think. But I don't say it.

"Yeah. I just... why now? I thought that we weren't ever talking again. You made it pretty clear how you felt when things ended."

Emily went a little pink. "I was really angry with you. Not my finest moment, I'll give you. Still, I think that you've had some time to see the error of your ways..."

I grit my teeth, even though she is completely right. I know I was in the wrong, without a doubt. But that knowledge doesn't come from me being... *semi*-alone... for almost five months. The two aren't related.

Or are they?

"Right," I say abruptly. I don't really have time to sit

and philosophize this question right now. I have food to cook, for a girl who couldn't be more different than Emily.

Yeah, a girl that you're not sure even likes you, I think. I have a mild freak out, ending the conversation with Emily. "I have to get going. It's nice seeing you."

"Call me," she says, looking worried.

I just wave in her direction, getting into my car as quickly as I can. I pull out, leaving Emily still standing there, making a confused face.

I can appreciate the fact that she's wondering what the hell is going on with me, because I sure as fuck don't know. Here I am, getting groceries to try to woo the girl I'm... seeing, or whatever... and there is Emily, sweet and pleasant and eager to please.

Cady could not be more different than Emily. She seems smart, yet difficult and obstinate. Even their looks are completely opposite. Emily is like a sweet bit of fluff that you know will probably give you a stomach ache. Cady offers a deeper, more satisfying connection, but only if you can get her to let you in.

Based on the sex alone, I'd be crazy to pick anyone but Cady. And obviously if there were a relationship, I'd rather date Cady. But if I were going on the ease of connecting, the natural lightness of it, I would consider Emily.

That might just be laziness, though. I honestly don't know.

I pull into the driveway of my house, a majestic-looking white brick two story affair. I turn off my car, then take a few deep, calming breaths.

You are going to text Cady, and you're going to make dinner for her. The rest of the shit you have in your head just has to go somewhere else, in a secret black box that is compartmentalized from everything else.

I pull out my phone and text Cady my address. A few seconds later, I hear back from her.

Where is that?

You'll have to find out, won't you? I'm here right now, and I have something special planned for you.

Should I wear anything in particular or bring anything?

Just bring yourself and that amazing ass. I have plans for it tonight.

Oh really? I'm intrigued. I'll be there in about half an hour.

I get out of the car, carrying the groceries into the house and depositing them in the massive white-tiled chef's kitchen. It's a shame that I don't usually cook much, because I think that this kitchen is a cool space. Going around the huge butcher block kitchen island, I put everything away in the Viking fridge.

I go upstairs to change my shirt, opting for a basic black button up to go with my jeans. I take my boots off, preferring to go barefoot in my own house.

When Cady rings the doorbell, I hurry down to the front door. I open it, grinning at her perplexed expression.

"Is this your house?" she says, looking at the uniform bricks and ivy-covered wrought iron accents. I eye her tight pastel pink dress and black heels appreciatively.

"Ding ding ding," I say, stepping back and sweeping a hand to lead her inside. "Is it not what you imagined?"

She laughs as she steps in. "Not even a little bit. I pictured you having one of those fancy condos downtown, for some reason. Oh my god, this place is amazing."

She's wide eyed as I give her a brief tour. "This is the kitchen. This is the library, although I never spent any time here. Here's the living room…"

I bring her into the living area, a couple of white leather couches clustered around a big screen tv. Like the rest of the house, it's done with a lot of cedar accents and white walls, only interrupted here and there by well-chosen art.

In other words, I had very little to do with decorating this room.

"I had no idea that your house was so... fashionable," she says.

"I just picked out the television," I admit. "The rest of it was an interior designer named Justin."

"I see," she says, putting her purse down beside one of the couches. "This is all very illuminating."

"Is it?" I ask, taking her hand and drawing her close. I kiss her, and her lips are as sweet as anything I've ever tasted.

Her hands come up and link behind my neck. I love that she's still so much smaller than me, that I can dominate her so easily. I slide my hands around her waist, then cup and knead her ass.

It's difficult not to get pulled in so fast, but I eventually manage to make myself back off.

"I have a surprise for you," I say, kissing her on the lips a final time before releasing her.

"Yeah?" she says, a flicker of carnal interest in her eyes.

"Come on," I say. "Come to the kitchen. I'm making you a meal."

"What?" she says, taken aback. "Like... actual food?"

I lead her by the hand on the way back to the kitchen, chuckling.

"Yep." I pull out one of the stools sitting under the butcher block kitchen island for her. "Sit."

She looks curious; I'll take what I can get, as long as she is willing to play along. I grab an apron out of a drawer, unfolding it with a shake. I turn the oven on, then show off my apron to her.

"Kiss The Cook?" Cady says, amused. "I plan on doing plenty of that tonight."

"I wasn't kidding when I said I had plans for you later," I say, hunting down a sheet pan. I pick a spatula out and point it at her. "After the salmon is done, though."

"Ooooh, salmon?" she says. I hear one of her shoes drop to the floor, then the other.

I turn away, hiding a smug grin over the fact that she's getting comfy in my house. I don't want to point that out though, it might scare her off.

"Yeah," I say. "And asparagus, and fresh bread. You're getting spoiled tonight."

She cocks her head. "Any particular reason?"

"Because I couldn't watch you eat out of one more goddamn takeout container," I say, grinning at her. "I'm onto you, you know. You're going to have to eat reasonable meals if you have a kid."

Her lips thin out as she presses them together. I recognize this look of repressed outrage; Emily used to give me this look all the time. "Oh, you're the expert now, are you?"

I open the fridge and get the salmon and asparagus out, then arrange them on the baking sheet.

"No, I'm just a guy that wants to feed a girl he likes some decent food."

I glance at her, and I'm glad I did, because she is blushing so damned hard at my words.

"You're ridiculous," she mutters, rolling her eyes. It doesn't matter, though, because I can see that she is pleased and flustered.

I grab the salt and pepper and hit the fish and asparagus, then put it in the oven. I take the bread out of its bag and leave it on the oven to warm it up.

"So has anything interesting happened to you in the last two days?" Cady asks.

I freeze for a second, my mind flashing back to the Whole Foods parking lot. I know that's not what she is talking about, but it is certainly the most interesting thing to happen to me in the last forty-eight hours.

I straighten up, turning to look at her. "What do you mean?"

"I mean… tell me what's going on, you know? In your life." She gives me an odd look.

Man, do I feel guilty. I feel like I did something dirty, hiding a filthy secret from her. Except, I haven't done anything. As far as I know, we're not even exclusive. And all I did was talk to Emily.

I'm making too much of this, I can tell. "I don't know. I've just been working, mostly."

"Ah. Well, I have some office gossip that's pretty good," she says, breezily. "My big boss and his secretary apparently got caught in the supply closet together. Everybody is in a complete tizzy about it. Even Olive cares, apparently, though I don't know why. I hardly got anything done today because people kept stopping by to *chat*."

She uses air quotes on the last word, rolling her eyes. She looks at me, expecting some kind of reaction, and I manage a smile.

"That's pretty good," I say. "Last year, my boss's wife left him for a lady in accounting, and everyone was aghast."

"Oooooh, that's juicy!" Cady says with a laugh. "How long did the gossip last?"

"Way too long." I get a block of butter out of the fridge.

Cady keeps the conversation going, chatting about where she wants to go on vacation later this year. I feel super weird and shady about the whole Emily thing. It would just be so much better if we had clear boundaries.

I turn around, crossing my arms. "I have to ask you something."

Her brows shoot up. "Okay. What?"

"Are you sleeping with anyone else?"

Her expression is priceless. "Me? No. Why, are you?"

I'm beyond relieved. I drop my arms. "Uh… no."

"Oh. I mean, I didn't think it needed to be said, but… yeah, only one guy at a time for me."

"Okay. I was just checking," I say, shrugging as if it's not a big deal.

"Uh huh…" she says, hopping down off the stool.

She comes around the island, reaching up for me. Her kiss is bold, and her hands wander over my ribs, squeeze the thick vee of muscle at my hips. I press against her, my cock thickening. She makes a soft, needy noise.

I lift her up by her ass, savoring the feel of her legs as they wrap around me. I move slowly, first turning off the oven, and then carrying her out of the kitchen altogether.

The salmon is forgotten as we lose ourselves in each other.

CADY

I get home late from work, late enough that the sun is already set. A stress headache brews between my eyebrows, threatening to unleash itself at at moment. Flinging my keys and my overstuffed tote bag full of briefs down, I head straight to the closet.

Milo looks on curiously as I kick off my heels and change out my black sheath dress for yoga pants and an oversized off-the-shoulder sweat shirt.

I stop and sit on the bed for a few minutes, giving Milo affection. He meows the whole time, which usually makes me smile, but at the moment my head feels like it's about to burst.

"Hey, Little Prince," I coo at him, rubbing him behind his ears. "Please, please, please be quiet."

He finally lies down, presenting his tummy to me. He's purring like crazy, which always makes me happy. I grab one of his toys, a fake bird on a string, and play with him until he loses interest. When he gets tired, he gets up and stalks away.

"You just be like that," I tell him. "Act like you don't love me."

Milo looks back at me quizzically. I get up and head for the kitchen. I feel this headache looming, throbbing at the base of my head, all the way up to my crown.

On top of everything else, I took a pregnancy test this morning. Of course, I knew that it couldn't be positive. Not yet. But seeing the two lines on the test made me frown.

I think about having a glass of wine, because I am definitely not fucking pregnant, but that might actually make my headache worse.

I grab a big glass of water, and get my phone from my tote bag. A text from Jett waits, as it usually does these days.

What are you doing?

I bite my lower lip. I'm in absolutely no mood for sex, that's for certain.

I have the worst headache.

I have something for that.

I narrow my eyes. *Don't take this the wrong way, but I am not interested in your cock right now.*

lolololol. No, something else. It's a plant, and it's illegal.

I pause, my brow hunching. Is he talking about marijuana?

Do you mean 🌿?

Yeah. I have a bunch of brownies in my freezer. I'd be happy to bring you one.

I think about it, then use my phone to Google 'is it safe to eat pot brownies when you're trying to conceive?' The results are totally mixed, but most of them say that it's relatively safe.

I purse my lips and reply.

I don't know… I've only had 🌿 once, at a party. I puked everywhere.

I guarantee you won't puke AND that your headache will go away.

Promise?

I promise. Be there soon.

I set my phone down, and gulp the water down. I head into the kitchen and drink two more glasses, even though I don't want to. When Jett arrives, I am laying on the couch, my arm thrown over my eyes.

He buzzes at the door, and I blearily get up and let him in. As I am waiting for him to come up, I wonder how weird it would be to just give him the door code and the key. I wonder if that would be weird, since I'm not his girlfriend or anything.

Might as well be, though. He hangs out with me nearly every night I'm free, and he's bringing me headache relief at the moment.

The thought gets derailed a bit when he arrives, looking his usual handsome self in jeans and a dark grey button up shirt. His hair is a little shorter, and his beard has been trimmed more than usual.

"Hey you," he says, casually dropping a kiss on my head and hugging me.

"Did you get your hair cut?" I ask, enjoying how delicate and small he makes me feel with his embrace. "Here, come sit. I was just sprawled on the couch."

He collapses on the couch, pulling me down with him, so I'm partially sprawled out on top of him. I don't mind at all, except I wish that my head wasn't throbbing like crazy.

"I did get a haircut. Thanks for noticing." He wiggles his eyebrows, pulling a white paper bag from his back pocket. "I brought your weed brownie."

"Ehhhh," I say. "I'm still not sure about it. You're not going to make me do it alone, are you?"

He looks thoughtful. "Well, I brought plenty, but…"

"But what?" I say, pouting.

"If I have some, I can't drive."

I look at him, confused. "So?"

"So I couldn't drive home, is my point that I'm trying to make," he finishes.

"Oh! You mean you'd just… sleep over?"

"I would have to, yeah."

"Well, do that! I mean… I'm asking you. Will you sleep over and eat a pot brownie with me?"

Jett gives me that million-dollar smile of his. "Of course."

He pulls out the brownie, putting a quarter of it into my cupped hands.

"There, that's a good place to start," he judges. "You can always eat more, but you don't want to overdo it."

I give him a half smile, then eat it. To my surprise, it's actually good, really dense and moist and chocolatey. He eats a little too, then wraps the rest up and puts it aside.

"We should probably go lay down in the bedroom," he suggests. "I'll rub your head, too, if that sounds good."

I look at him, suddenly feeling very grateful. "Thank you for doing all of this, Jett. I know you didn't have to come over. You don't have to give me a scalp massage on top of that."

I can tell that there is something on his mind, something that he wants to say, but he doesn't. He just gives me a quick hug, and I don't push him to speak. He guides me off the couch, turning off the living room lights. The bedroom is dark, and I sink onto the mattress with a sigh.

Jett lays down beside me, and gently turns me onto my stomach. I feel silly and childish, letting him do something so... I don't know, intimate? But as soon as he buries his big hands in my hair, wrapping them around my skull, I let out a breath I didn't know I had been holding.

He rubs my scalp in little circles, slowly releasing tiny knots of tension and kneading away my worries. When he wraps his hands around the base of my skull again and rubs my neck with his thumbs, I let out a moan of pleasure.

My whole body begins to feel tingly and good. It's minor at first, but then I feel it more and more. My headache is long gone, completely forgotten. I become acutely aware of how soft my bed is under my body, of how silky and smooth my coverlet feels against my skin.

Jett moves down to my shoulders, and I gasp. He chuckles, and I can feel his laughter where his skin touches mine. "I'm guessing the pot is kicking in?"

"Uh huh," I say, nodding slowly. "Yeah, I think so."

"How is your head?" he asks.

"Amazing. I mean... I forgot that I was about to get a migraine," I sigh. I roll over under his hands, my sweatshirt slipping a little lower to show my entire shoulder. "This feels so good."

He grins, reaching out to trace a figure eight on my collarbone. "Yep. I don't eat brownies very often, but it's always great when I do."

I smile at him, propping myself up on one arm. "We should do something. Wait, no. We should talk about like... the truths of the universe or something."

Jett lifts his brows. "The truths of the universe?"

"Yeah," I say, reaching out to run my fingertips along his arm. "Or... how about personal truths?"

"Personal truths? Like what?" he asks, catching my wandering hand and interlacing our fingers.

I look at our hands together, at how small my fingers are next to his, and have a lightbulb moment.

"I think one of the reasons that I'm so attracted to you, your body at least, is how dainty you make me feel," I say, not really answering his question.

"Oh yeah?" he says. "Is that a personal truth?"

"No, more of an observation." I look at him, at his dark blue eyes, dark hair, and dark beard. "God, it is really stupid how attractive you are. It's unfair."

"Who says?" he says, grinning. "Besides, you get to have sex with me."

I bite my lip, grinning at Jett. "That is very true. You know what I wonder about you?"

"No. Do tell." He lets go of my hand and brushes a piece of my hair into place.

"I want to know why you have so many tattoos. Not that I don't like them, but... I have to imagine that they hurt. Especially these ones." I trace several cherry blossoms that are tattooed on the side of his neck, reaching from his ear down to the collar of his dark grey shirt.

He seems to enjoy my touch, taking my hand in his again and kissing my palm.

"That's a good question," he says. "My first one was the crest on my chest. It represents family to me, or... the bond that Jax and I have."

"Jax is your brother, right?"

"Yeah. It means a lot to me to know that even though my mom was fucked up, the James name stands for a lot more than just her. It's about the unbreakable bond that a family should offer, if that makes any sense."

My eyes widen. His words make me wonder why he doesn't have a family of his own yet. "I didn't know that you had such strong feelings about family."

He shrugs. "My feelings about my family are complicated. Anyway, once I got the crest, I got hooked. I like the pain, and the sacrifice it takes to get a tattoo. Now that I have full sleeves, I just get a little more added every year. I think that my next tattoo is going to be right here."

He smoothes his hand over a spot on his ribs. I touch the spot after him.

"Can I see?" I say.

He gives me an odd look. "It doesn't have any ink yet."

"I'm just trying to get you to take off your shirt," I say playfully. "Is that so wrong?"

"Oh, well in *that* case," he says, sitting up and unbuttoning his shirt. He takes it off and then reclines again, and I trace his chest tattoos with a finger. He smirks. "Is that better?"

I blush. "Maybe. And by that I mean, yes."

Jett puts his arm around my waist, pulling me flush against his body. He looks down into my eyes, and when he speaks his voice is gravelly. "I can't believe you still blush for me. Will you always do that, I wonder?"

My immediate thought is, *at least until I have your baby… because you won't want me after that. Not when I'm fat and pregnant and crazy.*

The thought that I'm willingly going to walk away from him someday soon has my heart breaking. I realize that I might really be falling for Jett, even though he's supposed to just be my sperm donor.

But he kisses me senseless in the next moment, before I have a chance to voice anything. I sigh into his kiss, ripples of sensation tripping up and down my spine. He slides his hand into my hair, gripping it, and I gasp.

Everything else falls away in that moment, forgotten.

JETT

I'm naked, stoned, and I have Cady riding me like my name is fucking Seabiscuit. I grip her hips as she works her whole body up and down, back and forth.

God damn.

She's so fucking good that if I think about it for too long, my toes start to clench and I get really really close to coming.

So I force myself to relax and breathe, to feel her incredible pussy and let her be in control. She's bracing both her hands on my chest, digging her nails into my flesh. I'm loving every goddamned second of it.

My eyes keep bouncing between how amazing her tits look as she moves and the open-mouthed expression of pure pleasure on her face. Her eyes are squeezed shut as she moves up and down on my cock, concentrating very hard.

Every once in a while she says, "fuck!", which I take as a compliment. I can feel her core tightening like a spring, contracting rhythmically. She's close.

I slide my hand down across my stomach to my cock. I

manage to get my thumb positioned so that it hits her clit hard every time she comes down. Her eyes open, so perfectly grey that it's almost startling. Cady looks right at me.

"Yes," she says, her hips working hard and fast. "God, Jett. Right there! You're going to make me cum so hard…"

I can feel my balls tensing up, feel my toes curling at little. "Fuck, Cady. You're so fucking tight. Don't stop!"

She comes apart at the seams, her pussy clenching and spasming. I let go of the tiny bit of control I have left as soon as I feel her come, bucking up into her body, pulsing jets of hot cum into her. She drains me dry. I imagine her greedy little body sucking up every last drop.

Cady falls onto my chest, struggling for breath. I wrap an arm around her, appreciating the warmth of her body atop mine. It feels like we lie there trying to catch our breath for ages, but it's probably only a few minutes.

I push some of Cady's hair out of my face, but then I feel bad that I pushed it onto her forehead. Using both of my hands, I try and fail to get the long black mass to behave.

"You having fun there?" she asks, grinning.

"No. I give up." I ruffle her hair so it looks crazier than ever, and she gives me a playful slap on the chest. I laugh at her reaction. "You're cute when you're feisty."

"Alright," she says, carefully extricating herself from my body. "I'm frigging starving."

"What? A stoner with the munchies? Unheard of," I tease, sitting up. I know I have to go to her bathroom and wash up, but I'm feeling really lazy.

"I don't think I have anything here," she pouts. "You should have warned me!"

I glance at the clock on her bedside table. "It's eleven,

so takeout isn't going to happen. What's close enough to walk to?"

"Mmmm... nothing, really. Oh! Actually... there is a Waffle House a few blocks from here. Those are all twenty four hours a day, seven days a week."

"Really? Do you hang out there a lot?" I kid her.

"No. But I'm willing to take a gamble. Anything that is covered with cheese sounds amazing right now."

"Hmmm. Okay, I'm game if you are. Just give me a minute to clean myself up here."

I get up and go to her bathroom, washing myself off a bit. She has her clothes on when I get out, and we trade places. I get dressed in her bedroom, then wander into the kitchen.

There on the kitchen counter are printouts of the pictures Olive insisted on taking that day at the Orpheus brewery. Unbeknownst to me, there is one of just me and Cady. My arm is slung around her shoulders, and she is looking at me admiringly.

If it were someone else, a strange couple, I would say that she looks at him with love in her eyes. *If* it were someone else who wasn't... *her*.

Picking the photo up, my heart gives a funny squeeze as I look at us together. We make a really good looking couple, me with my dark hair and tattoos and her with her long braid and red lipstick.

This feeling, the one I'm having right now? This feeling says that I should have just asked her to be my girlfriend, rather than asking if she was sleeping with anyone else. This feeling tells me to do all kinds of things, pin her to the floor and fuck her until she says she loves me.

I drop the photo, turning away from the counter with a frown.

There's one issue with that scenario. The big question that neither of us knows how to ask.

What happens to the two of us when she finds out she's pregnant? Does it change everything? Will I still be able to walk away, scot free, if I want to?

Contractually, I'm honestly not sure. All I know is that my gut tells me that Cady is mine, but I have no idea what Cady actually wants.

I hear a meow, and turn toward the living room to see Milo peering around the couch. He's checking me out, maybe seeing if I'm good enough for Cady. I walk over and Milo moves to the other end.

I sit down, and hold out my hand. Milo sniffs the air around me delicately, and comes up to my hand. He looks at me pointedly, but when I move my hand to try to pet him, he gets scared.

Milo and I both look up when Cady comes in the room, looking very put together for someone who is baked out of her mind. She's brushed her hair and teeth, and swapped her outfit from earlier for high-waisted jeans and a bright yellow crop top.

"All that just to go get waffles?" I ask, looking her up and down. "Don't get me wrong, I'm not complaining, but that is a lot of work."

She flashes me a smile. "I'm just trying to keep up with you, mister I'm Always So Put Together."

"Alright, alright," I say. "Are you ready to go?"

Cady nods, grabbing her wallet and her phone off the counter. We head downstairs and out into the warm evening air, talking and laughing as we go.

"No, listen!" she insists as we walk across the dingy, poorly lit parking lot of Waffle House. I look up at the bright yellow and black sign as we hit the door. "I think that you're just not listening to the right Katy Perry songs. She's great."

"Uh huh," I say.

I'm distracted for a moment as we enter the tiny diner. It's brightly lit and mostly empty, two rows of booths, a counter with seats, and behind all that is the grill. It smells straight up like french fries, and it's kept super cold to suit the couple of employees who are working the grill.

"Sit anywhere that's clean," a young woman tells us, holding bread over a toaster just behind the booths. "I'll be right with y'all."

I hold out my hand, indicating to Cady that she can choose where we sit. She picks the closest booth, and slides in one side. I sit on the other side, cringing at how low to the ground the booths are.

"Hey!"

I look to my right, and there is Emily, all bubbly and blonde. Of all fucking people to be at this Waffle House right now, she's the one person I want to see least. I'm pretty sure I had a nightmare about Emily and Cady meeting, and I'm still shaking after that one.

"Oh. Hey Emily," I say, already starting to sweat.

I try not to convey my desperate wish to be anywhere else to Cady, but I'm obviously not successful. Cady sticks out her hand to Emily.

"Hi. I'm Cady." She looks as strong and confident as one can while stoned, in a Waffle House, and sitting two feet below the person standing.

"Emily," Emily says, taking Cady's measure. "I'm Jett's ex-girlfriend."

"Mmm! Interesting," Cady says. "He's never mentioned you."

My brows rise. This is a lie; I told Cady about Emily on the night we met. Unless she's forgotten, Cady is being kind of catty right out of the gate. I don't say shit. There is nothing that I can say that makes me look good.

"Really? That's strange. We saw each other a couple of days ago. Didn't we, Jett?"

Emily and Cady both look at me. Cady is looking at me with a hint of the wounded animal that she's hiding inside. Emily smiles, because she's managed to score a point on Cady. And me?

I am truly fucked.

"We ran into each other in the grocery store parking lot," I say flatly. "You make it sound like we had a date or something."

"Well, we do!" Emily fires back. "Remember? The fun run?"

I glance at Cady, who has gone as still as stone. I shake my head at Cady, but I know that's not going to unring the bell.

"Hey, don't look at me. I'm not your girlfriend," Cady snaps.

My palms sweat. She is right about that.

"I didn't agree to that," I say to Emily. "At all."

Emily smirks. "Well, that fun run is coming up soon. You have my number still, don't you? Or did you forget that, too?"

Cady crosses her arms and glares at Emily.

"Bye, Emily," I bite off.

Emily just smirks and heads out of the diner.

"I can't believe her," I steam. Cady looks off into the distance with an irritable expression.

The waitress comes up, her order pad at the ready. "Y'all know what ya want?"

I look at Cady, then pick up the menu, which doubles as a placemat. I order a waffle and eggs, and Cady orders a waffle and some bacon. When the waitress is gone again, I look at Cady.

"Hey," I say, grabbing one of her hands. "Look at me."

When she looks at me, pulling her hand away, there are tears shining in her enormous grey eyes. She dabs at her right eye, clearly embarrassed to be emotional in front of me.

"She was just trying to get the best of you," I say.

"Yeah, well, she did a pretty good job of it." Cady wipes away another tear. She's eying the door like she's about to bolt from the diner altogether.

Shit. That look on her face? That is one hundred percent my fault.

"I'm trying to figure out how I could have stopped this from happening. I don't want to be the reason that you feel bad," I say.

Cady takes a deep breath, then releases it. "It's nothing. There isn't anything you could have done. It's not a big deal."

"If you want, I can start telling you… I don't know, boyfriend stuff," I finish lamely.

She glances at me sharply. "Boyfriend stuff?"

"Yeah. I mean… since we are only sleeping with each other, it kind of makes sense that—"

I don't get the chance to finish. She pushes herself up and out of the booth, shaking her head. "I need to go home and go to bed."

"What about our food?" I say, looking around.

"I'm just tired, okay? Please, Jett. Let's go." She does look totally drained, with dark pouches under her eyes.

"Of course, yeah." I slide out of the booth, pulling out my wallet and throwing a twenty on the table. We walk back to her apartment in silence. Halfway there, she puts her hand in mine and leans on my arm.

I'm at a total fucking loss right now. Though I am sure that she's going to kick me out, she doesn't. She just heads to bed, crawling under the covers. I settle in, uncertain what to expect.

Cady rolls over on her side and pulls me close, so that I roll over and spoon her. We both lie there for the longest time, not talking. My mind is whirling, going over and over everything that's been said tonight.

One thing is for certain: Cady does *not* like talking about her feelings or showing weakness in front of me.

She cut me off when I offered to be more… boyfriend-like, by sharing stuff with her. There is only so much I can do to make a relationship work; she has to meet me halfway, or there isn't really any point.

I stare into the darkness until sleep takes me over.

CADY

I'm at work, deep in a stack of briefs, going over them with a pen and a highlighter. I frown and flip to the next page. I rock back in my desk chair, looking up at the glass wall of my office as some lawyers pass.

I look back at the legal brief, but it starts to blur before my eyes. I put it down on the desk and sigh. I have been working on this for hours, and it's almost time to go home.

I'm supposed to hang out with Jett at some party of his extended friend circle. I must have agreed to it when I was high, because it doesn't sound like something that a future baby mama should be attending.

No, it sounds like just the sort of thing he would bring his girlfriend to, if he had a girlfriend. But he doesn't; he has me instead.

I won't even begin to address the issues that thinking about that brings up for me. All my feelings are so tangled up and entwined, and that is before I even add the *idea* of a baby to the mix.

A knock comes at my office door, and I look up to find Helen Master there. The third most powerful attorney in our firm and a hell of a litigator, Helen looks immaculate in her crisp white pantsuit.

She's not someone who drops by for casual chats; I mostly see her once a month at litigation-specific firm meetings. She pokes her head in.

"Hi, can I come in?" she asks.

"Of course!" I say, looking askance at my desk and office chairs, which are covered with legal briefs. "Sorry, I can clear one of these off for you…"

I hop up, but Helen just smiles. "No. I will close the door, though, if that's alright."

I am already jittery from all the coffee I've had this morning. Now I start to sweat a little. I can't help it.

"Sure, sure," I say. I go ahead and clear off a chair, and Helen perches on the arm.

"I can see you're busy, so I'll be quick." Helen smiles. "I've noticed that you are a real go-getter, especially on this Greenway vs. Taylor case that we've all been working on. You've logged an absolutely crushing number of hours in the last few months, and it hasn't gone unnoticed."

I think of all the nights that I could have gone a little longer, stayed a little later, but I didn't because I had someone waiting for my call. My cheeks color. "Thanks."

"We are looking at starting a branch of our firm in Seattle, and we could use some good people there. People like you. I would like for you to run the litigation department for us in Seattle." Helen sits back, self-satisfied.

My mouth opens, but no words come out. She wants me to move to Seattle? And run their litigation department? I'm flabbergasted. "I— I— Can I think about it?"

Helen cocks her head, as if curious why anyone would say such a thing.

"Well, certainly," she says. "You probably have a month to decide. Take some time, sleep on it… but don't take too much time. There are a ton of people who would love to have this kind of opportunity. Oh, and this is sort of hush-hush, so... please don't tell anyone at the firm."

She stands up, moving toward the door.

"Thank you, Helen. I'm honestly so blown away," I manage.

"Bye, Cady." She gives me a small smile, and then lets herself out of my office.

I sit back in my chair, legal briefs momentarily forgotten. I've never been offered such a big promotion in my life. The benefits to moving and opening the Seattle office would be huge, I'm sure of it. But the promotion might be jeopardized by the fact that I'm actively trying to get pregnant right now.

I chew on my lower lip. I can't not go for it though, can I? That would be stupid.

I need advice. Jett's face pops into my mind. The next thing I know, I'm imagining having to leave Jett behind.

My eyes start tearing up at the very thought. I've done a great job of ignoring any and all feelings I have about him since that night at Waffle House, though. Just shut it down with a smile, and distracted him with sex. So far, it works.

I glance at the big clock on the wall and realize that I have to get going if I'm going to meet Jett. I hurry to tidy my desk, and then grab my stuff and get out of there.

I am meeting Jett at a restaurant in Buckhead, some little place that his friends all know. On my way over, I look down at my pale pink blouse and white pants. It's probably a little fancy for the occasion. I unbutton a couple buttons and sigh. There honestly isn't much else I can do.

I pull into the parking lot of the restaurant, a little wooden building that leans a bit alarmingly. I'm surprised to see Jett standing outside, looking dapper in all black.

When he sees me, his whole face lights up. I don't want to admit it, but I am coming to live for those moments.

God, I am so emotionally fucked right now, it's not even funny.

Still, I get out of the car, walking up to Jett. He's looking me up and down like I'm chocolate cake, and he just got the last piece.

"You look fucking hot," he says, hugging me tightly. I bury my face against his chest for a second, and breathe him in.

He always smells like pine and soap. I liked it before; now I think I love the way he smells.

Oh god, too many emotions, I think, pushing them back. Not right now.

"You smell good," I say.

"Thanks, I remembered to shower," he jokes. He pulls back, and I can tell from his expression that he wants to ask me something. "So, um... I might have... told everybody inside that you were my girlfriend."

He winces before I can even respond. I look at him, indecisive. We have been dancing around this subject for weeks now, and I'm too tired to put up much of a fight. A secret, dark part of me is even pleased, if I'm honest with myself.

Jett is looking at me, holding his breath.

"Okay," I finally say, shrugging. "If that's what you want to call me."

The surprise is evident in his expression. "Really?"

"Yes. As long as our agreement about... the baby... still stands, I can be your girlfriend."

He genuinely beams at me, closing in for a kiss. He cups my face tenderly, and his kiss is hot and slow. When he breaks the kiss, he leans his forehead against mine for a moment.

For the first time, I start to wonder how Jett feels. Is he feeling the magnetic pull between the two of us? It can't just be me, not if he told his friends I was his girlfriend.

Jesus, I am horrible for not considering his feelings sooner.

He makes a face. "You should be aware, this is a bridal shower sort of thing. For the couple that is getting married in like a week and a half? So there will be lots of my friends here, plus some kids too."

"I didn't know! You're supposed to bring a gift to these things!" I protest.

"Lucky you, I picked something off the registry. They're getting really nice set of Le Creuset dishes, I guess. You can piggyback on my gift. Ready to go inside?"

I nod, and he whisks me into the restaurant. It's a tiny Italian place, and every surface is made of mismatched old wood. We go straight past the empty hostess stand and several tables laden with delicious-looking, garlicky food. The party of fifty or so people is a bit subdued, with everyone standing around and chatting in small groups.

There are probably ten kids playing in a side room, ranging from toddlers to elementary school age. My heart melts when a toddler runs by me, chased by a pretty blonde who was probably her mother.

"Hey, you came!"

I turn and see that Mason is surrounded by a group of women. His megawatt smile tells me that's a good thing. He beckons us over.

"Cady, this is everybody," Mason says. "Alice, Bea, Emmie, Sarah, and Gretchen."

The girls all smile and greet me with waves. A couple of them say hi. I'm sort of awkward, but Jett jumps in and saves me.

"This is my girlfriend, Cady," Jett says. Mason gives him a look, but I'm not privy to whatever that's about.

"Hi," I say, waving to them all. "It's nice to meet you guys."

Jett puts his arm around my waist. "We should go say hi to the couple of the hour."

We approach a young couple who are chatting animatedly with an older couple. I look at the engaged couple, and see their happiness written plain all over their faces. It's hard not to find their glee contagious.

Jett waits until the right moment to interject. "Hey, guys. Danny, Mary, this is Cady. Cady, this is Mary and Danny. I've known Mary since college, if you'd believe that. They are getting married."

I lean forward to shake both their hands. "It's a pleasure!"

"Honestly, the pleasure is mine," Mary says. "I'm so glad to get to meet Jett's girlfriend. I was getting worried about him for a minute there."

I laugh. "I'm worried now, honestly."

"Here, come on, let's get you a glass of wine," Mary commands. "You can tell me about yourself."

I let her escort me to the bar, and sip a bit of red wine. We chat about our jobs a little. Mary is a thousand times more enthusiastic about everything than anyone I'm friends with, which I find charming.

I keep track of Jett out of the corner of my eye. It's not long before Jett is playing with a couple of the little girls, dancing with them and cracking them up. My heart starts to hurt, in the best possible way. He's a complete natural with kids, doing a wacky dance and dissolving them into a pile of giggles.

"He's good with kids," Mary says, nodding at him. "You're lucky. Danny is super awkward around kids."

I bite my lip, unsure how to respond. Yeah, he might be good with kids... and he might be fathering my baby... but doing the math there is just too much to ask of me right now.

"Omigod, I'm sorry," Mary says, rolling her eyes at herself. "I didn't mean... I've had too much wine to talk to people, probably."

"It's not even a thing," I wave her off. "And you're right, I am lucky."

I smile at Mary, while I keep watching Jett out of the corner of my eye. This is the problem right here, I think. He makes me feel so friggin good. He's checking all the boxes for what I want in a future mate... but I'm putting the cart before the horse, trying to have a baby while I tentatively start to date him.

I know that what I feel for Jett is foolish. When I'm fat and pregnant, he won't want anything to do with me anymore. But right now, looking at him as he slow dances with the youngest of the girls, moving around with her on his feet... my heart is going insane.

Telling me that I love him.

Telling me to say aloud something, anything, about how I feel.

Sipping my wine, I wonder if this is how my mom felt about my dad, right before child protective services took me away. For the first time in a long time, I desperately wish that she were around so I could ask.

After a while, Jett comes over to me. He is so tall and dashing, I can't stand it.

"Having fun?" he asks, swooping in for a kiss.

"Yeah. Mary is nice," I say, smiling.

"She is. Her fiancé is great too."

"Mmhm. It was fun watching you dance with the girls over there," I say, nodding at them.

His smile is easy. "Oh yeah. I've known Melanie and Jamie literally since they were born. I like playing uncle Jett."

"You seem really natural with kids," I say, swirling the wine in my glass. "Why don't you have any kids?"

Jett slides me a gaze. "I've thought about it before. I just haven't found the right girl, I guess."

I don't know how to take that. Is he including me in his calculations when he says that? I wonder.

"And here I thought you were an irredeemable playboy, destined to break hearts forever," I tease.

I see that I've lost his attention. He's looking down my top at my cleavage. He pulls at the neckline just a hair, sneaking a peek.

"Really?" I whisper, batting at his hand.

"I can't help it. Your tits are looking fantastic tonight," he says with a shrug. "I can't wait to get you home and rip that shirt off of you."

I blush, but I can't help smiling. "You're terrible."

"You like it," he says, raising brow.

And he is right. I do like it.

In fact, I think I might love it.

JETT

I sit in the parking lot of Cure, a bar I've agreed to meet my brother Jax, Cady, Mason, and Alex at. I'm currently listening to the new Rae Sremmurd, and promising myself that I'll stay cool. I won't let him push my buttons.

See, Jax and I get along… for the most part. It's just better for our relationship now that he lives in L.A., and we rarely see each other. Because when Jax and I spend any kind of significant portion of time together, he starts to get on my nerves.

Mostly by doing shit like he did today. My brother just sprung this on me at the last minute, like everything he does in his life. He texted me a few hours ago to say that he would be in Atlanta for the night, and can he stay at my place?

I sigh. I always think that I'm a hot mess, but Jax takes the cake on that one. He's just lucky that he's a really good photographer, because without his art he's just a giant fucking asshole.

Getting out of the car, I check my reflection. Dark blue button up, black jeans, black boots. I smooth my beard down and muss my hair.

All my ducks are in a row. I head inside Cure, showing my identification to the bouncer at the door. It is dark inside, most of the light coming from the tall back wall of lit up shelves. The music is pretty loud for it only being seven thirty at night, heavy bass-tinged electropop coming through the speakers.

I spot Alex first, as usual. He's the easiest to pick out of a crowd, being a head taller than everyone else. He's standing at the bar, patiently waiting for the bartender to get to him.

"Hey, dude," Alex says as I sidle up alongside him.

"Hey. How's the hunt for a team?"

He grins. "The Dolphins and the Patriots are both flirting with me."

"That is fucking awesome!" I say. "That deserves a drink. What are you going to have?"

A flash of red catches my eye. I turn my head, and see Cady enter the bar. She's wearing a super short red dress, and white patent leather heels. She looks fucking delicious, miles and miles of bare legs on display. If I were a cartoon wolf, my eyes would look like hearts and my tongue would have rolled out like a carpet by now.

Then she sees me. My heart constricts when our eyes meet. She grins and strides over to us.

"Hi—" she starts. She barely gets the word out before I'm on her, dipping her back like a movie star for a kiss.

My arms are tight around her waist as I bend her backwards, my lips crushing hers. I catch a whiff of a little bit of vanilla and lavender, and I suck her scent into my lungs. If I could, I would devour Cady right here and now.

When I pull her upright, she wobbles for a second, a smile on her face. "Did you miss me or something?"

"Maybe," I say, smothering a grin.

I release her, but slap her on the ass playfully.

"Watch it," she says, threatening me with a single finger.

I grab her hand and return to Alex. "Sorry about that."

"Hi Alex," Cady says.

Alex gives us a lopsided grin and holds up a drink. "Don't worry about me."

"Are you telling me that I missed that bartender?" I say. "I'll never get her back, I'm afraid."

"Hey, there's Mason and Jax," Alex says, nodding to the door.

The two men come in, talking and smiling. Looking at Jax is like looking in the mirror, if I'd never decided to get a single tattoo and shaved regularly. He's exactly my height and has the same dark hair and blue eyes, but he's clean-shaven. Add the tight jeans and the white henley shirt, and you have an alternate version of me.

"Jett," Jax says, giving me a nod. "And... who is this?"

He looks at Cady, intrigue written all across his face. I see him look her up and down, and a curl of jealous protectiveness unfurls in my stomach.

"Hi, I'm Cady," she says, dropping my hand to shake his. "And you're Jax, I'm guessing?"

"The one and only." He holds her hand a bit too long, and for a second I swear he's going to kiss it. He glances at me and lets her go. "I'm assuming that my brother already filled you in?"

Cady surprises me by moving closer to me, and slipping an arm around me. "He did! All nice things, I assure you."

"There really aren't any bad things to say about me," Jax says.

"Alright, alright," I say. "You guys go grab one of those tables along the wall there, and Cady and I will get drinks."

"Beer for me," Mason says, heading over to a table.

Jax just says, "Old-fashioned." He follows Mason and Alex, leaving me and Cady to get drinks.

I put an elbow on the bar, waiting for the bartender. While I'm waiting, I glance at Cady. "Did I already tell you that you look fantastic?"

She blushes. I knew that she would, but that doesn't sap any of the pleasure from watching her cheeks go dark pink.

"Not in so many words, no," she says, biting her lower lip. I scope out her red lipstick admiringly; it's safe to say that I'll be wearing it later, from her mouth to mine. "You and Jax look exactly the same. Same eyes, same jawline…"

"Don't go falling in love with the guy," I say, teasing. "Whatever problems you think I have, he has them ten times worse."

She blushes again. "That's not what I meant. It's just… the family resemblance is so strong! I don't see that very often."

"My mom used to say that me and Jax looked exactly like our dad." I glance behind myself, and see that Jax is looking back at us, his expression unreadable.

"That makes sense," Cady says with a nod.

The bartender finally comes and takes our drink order. Soon we're heading for the table. Jax stands up and accepts his drink, then motions to the seat next to him. "Cady?"

She glances at me before taking the seat, leaving me to sit on her other side.

"You just flew three thousand miles to be here, but you're going to sit next to Cady?" I grouse.

"No offense, but you're not nearly as attractive as she

is," he says, sipping his cocktail. "Oh, would you look at that? She blushes much better than you do, brother."

"*She* doesn't like being talked about as if she's not here," Cady corrects him primly.

"I'm truly sorry," Jax says to Cady.

I move a little closer to Cady and put my arm around her. Jax smirks at my display of possessiveness, which gets to me. I grit my teeth, a muscle jumping in my cheek.

"Jax, what have you been up to in Los Angeles?" Alex asks.

"Uhhh, you know. This and that," Jax says, waving his hand. "I'm doing a series of celebrity photos at the moment, trying to get entertainers at their best. I'm actually in town to shoot Akon at a show he's doing here."

"Very cool," Mason says.

"Yeah. I think that we're going to go to Magic City strip club later, if you're interested. I'm sure that it would be a new experience for Cady." Jax winks at Cady. Her mouth turns down a little, indicating her distaste.

"I think we're good on that," I say.

A little part of me is pleased at Cady's reaction to Jax. Usually girls are wowed by his I'm a soulful artist bullshit. Or maybe that was just Emily?

"Your loss," Jax shrugs. "Hey, how is Emily these days?"

I glare at Jax, and Mason and Alex look uncomfortable. Cady, expressionless, stands up.

"I'm going to find the ladies' room," she says. She escapes before anyone else can say anything.

I turn to Jax. "What the fuck is wrong with you?"

He looks smug. "Nothing. I just wanted to know how your long term ex-girlfriend is. She always liked me. How did things end with you guys? Do you think that she be against me calling her?"

Before I know it, I'm up, with Jax pinned against the wall. My fist is raised, and I am ready to do my brother some serious harm.

"Hey, hey," Jax says, raising his hands. "I didn't realize that you were getting your jimmies so rustled."

"You have one chance," I say, getting in his face. "Stop harassing Cady, and stop bringing up things that will upset her." I can see the desire to argue on his face, so I shake him. "Seriously? Stop."

"Jesus, chill out. Just because you've finally found someone like mom to date—"

"What the fuck did you just say?" I raise my fist again.

"What? It's true. She looks just like mom. Dark hair, light eyes, kinda tall... and I don't doubt that she uses people like mom did, either."

I get really close to his face and whisper, "Fuck you. You don't know the first thing about Cady."

Alex clears his throat. "Guys? I think that we need to take this outside. The bartenders are looking at us."

Glancing back, I see that the bartenders are gathered in a group, looking at us and talking in low voices. I let go of Jax, and he immediately starts plucking at his shirt, like I disturbed it with my anger.

Cady comes back from the bathroom. Her wide eyed gaze takes us all in, and her brow hunches with worry.

"Is everything okay?" she asks, reaching for my hand.

I take her hand, reminding myself to calm the fuck down. "Yeah. I think we should go."

Jax looks a little sheepish. "Jett, man—"

"Bye, Jax," I tell him. To Alex and Mason, I say, "See you two later."

"Bye!" Cady says.

I haul her out of there, not happy until we're at my car. I'm not seeing red anymore, but I'm still close to the edge.

"Can we just take my car?" I ask.

"If you think you're okay to drive, then sure." Cady pulls me to a stop, hugging me. "I'm sorry your brother made you mad."

"No, I'm sorry. He shouldn't have asked about Emily. He was just trying to get a rise out of me," I say, shaking my head.

Cady pushes up on her tiptoes, dropping a light kiss on my lips. "Don't apologize for him. Besides, it just so happens that I wanted to get home in a hurry anyway."

She grabs my ass, surprising me into a laugh. I look down at her face, and she beams up at me.

"What?" she says. "I'm allowed to be horny. You're not the only one."

I kiss her again, slower this time. "Thank you."

"Come on, let's go," she says, separating herself from me.

She goes around to the passenger side, and I unlock the car. I see Jax standing before the entrance to Cure, watching us as we pull out of the parking lot. I ignore him, heading to the highway.

"Hey, do you want to stay at your house tonight?" Cady says.

I raise my eyebrows at her question. "Are you sure?"

"Mmmhm. I love my apartment, but there is something really nice about being in a house. Thought we could switch it up, get some variety."

I nod and pull onto the highway. "Sounds like plan."

She turns on the radio. Rap blares from the speakers, the new G-Eazy playing. I expect her to change it, but instead she just leans back and listens.

I just drive, trying not to let my experience with my brother stick with me. Besides, he's wrong about Cady being exactly like our mom. Cady is a successful lawyer with her own life and interests. She couldn't be further from mom if she tried.

I look over at Cady, who's staring off in the distance. I can't think about what Jax said tonight. I won't.

JETT

My phone buzzes on the hotel's fancy conference table. I look at it, desperate both to turn it off and to answer it. I do neither.

I've been in St. Louis for five days, golfing and buddying up to some of the higher-ups at my company. The thing is, I usually like these trips. I'm happy to get paid to eat and sleep somewhere new. I never have anything to look forward to back at home.

Except…

Now I do, a little. I mean, yeah, it's just sex. But apparently Cady must be missing me something fierce, because she has starting texting me a lot. And by texting, I mean sexting. And she's not just doing it over text, she's leaving me little voice memos of her breathing hard and moaning.

My phone buzzes again, and I break into a sweat. Mr. Wallace, the head of our company, stops what he's doing at the whiteboard and scowls at the dozen people sitting at the table.

Wallace is about a million years old. At the moment he

looks like he should be standing in his yard, yelling at us damn kids to stay the hell off of his lawn.

"Whose goddamn phone is that making so much racket?" he demands.

I sink lower into my seat, reaching for my phone. I flip it over and there are Cady's tits, front and center. I'm hard in a heartbeat.

Did I mention that she makes me fucking crazy?

My phone buzzes again as I am desperately try to turn it off, but it's too late. Wallace calls me out.

"James, who the hell is calling you?" he says.

"Err… I'm not sure," I say lamely. "Wrong number, maybe."

Wallace glares at me for a second more, then throws up his hands in disgust. "I forgot what the hell I was talking about. We'll have to pick this up tomorrow."

Someone flips on the lights, and the meeting breaks up. Stephen, who is sitting beside me, elbows me in the ribs.

"Is that your girl?" he asks, nodding toward my phone. "Because she has got one hell of a rack."

I roll my eyes and stand up. "She's none of your business."

"Wait, are you saying that she's single?" he teases. "Because I'm in the market, if you know what I mean."

"Shut up, dude," I say, heading for the door. I turn down the hall to head to my room, the opposite direction that everyone else is going.

"Are you skipping out on drinks and dinner to call her back?" Stephen calls, his voice mocking. "Someone's pussy whipped…"

I give him the middle finger without looking back. When I'm in the elevator alone, heading up, I feel safe looking at Cady's texts. I scan them, noticing that they get progressively more and more provocative.

I'm horny.

I miss the feel of your body, dominating mine. I miss your cock, the way it makes me feel so full.

And that piercing? I can feel it whenever you're inside me. Yeah, I miss that in particular.

Mmmm, I'm thinking about your cock sliding into my mouth.

I'm touching myself, and thinking about you fucking me.

Then a series of pics, starting with her tits, then her ass, and then a glorious shot of her pussy.

I'm done for the day, I text her. I'm almost to my room, where I can have some privacy.

I slip the phone in my pocket as I exit the elevator, heading along the hotel's red and yellow carpeting, passing rooms on my left and right. As I walk, I hear Stephen's voice in my head.

"Is that your girl?" he asks. "Are you saying that she's single?"

I don't know why I didn't tell him that Cady is my girlfriend. That's what I've been calling her, since Mary and Danny's bridal shower.

I get to my room and let myself in; it's a basic hotel room, nothing beyond a bathroom, a king sized bed, and a tv console. I kick off my shoes and loosen my tie, then peel off my jacket. My phone buzzes again as I lie down across the bed with a sigh. I check the screen.

Ready? it reads.

I use the video call feature, and the phone rings for a second, reflecting my own face back at me. Then Cady picks up. She's in her bed, with the lights low.

"Hey," she says, biting her lip. Her lipstick is that same perfect shade of red. Just looking at the color makes my cock stir.

"You've been very distracting today," I say lightly.

"Oh? Is that a good thing? Or have I been naughty?"

She pouts for a second, but I know that she's encouraged by my words.

"You've been very, very bad," I say. "You probably need to be punished."

Cady's eyes go wide. "Oh, but how will you do it from there?"

"Mmm, I'll just have to tell you what to do. If you don't do it exactly as I instruct, you'll have to wait until I get back to get off."

She grins. "Is that right?"

"Start by showing me what you're wearing," I say, shifting and getting comfortable on the bed.

She shows me that she's wearing a tiny white silk robe. "Like this?"

"Are you wearing anything beneath that robe?" I ask. I reach down and touch myself idly through my slacks; I'm fucking hard already, as always.

"Yes," she says, slowly pulling on the belt to show me what's underneath. "I'm wearing baby pink panties, and a matching bra."

"God, you are a bad girl," I tell her. "Let me see, can I see your nipples through your bra?"

She moves the camera a little, and sure enough, the bra is see-through. Her nipples stand at attention, begging for me to put them into my mouth.

"You're wearing too much," I tell her. "Take off the robe. And the bra, too."

Cady bites her lip teasingly as she takes her clothes off, leaving her in only panties. I am suddenly feeling suffocated by my dress shirt; I quickly strip off my tie and shirt, and I unbutton my slacks.

When I pick my phone back up, I'm treated to a closeup view of her tits as she positions her phone in an upright position. It's just far enough that I can see her face, her tits, and her hips at once. Eyeing that remaining scrap of light pink lace, I wonder what I should do next.

"Touch your breasts," I tell her. "Cup them. Play with your nipples."

She does, tugging hard on both her nipples at once. She moans as she pinches them, closing her eyes. "Mmmm, I wish you were touching them."

I reach into my boxer briefs, lazily stroking myself. "I wish I were eating your pussy. It's so sweet and fresh, and juicy as a fucking berry. Take those panties off and let me have a look."

Cady moves off camera for a second, and then repositions herself so that her pussy is close to the camera, her face further back. She spreads her lips, and I can see how fucking ready she is, dripping her juices onto the bed.

"*Fuckkkkk*," I groan. "Is that for me? Are you fucking wet for me, princess?"

"Yes," she says, her voice breathy. "God, I want you so bad."

"Mmm. Show me with your fingers where you would want my mouth."

She slowly dips two fingertips into her core, and draws them back up to her clit. She moans softly. "Like this?"

"Jesus christ," I say. "Yes, just like that."

I stop for a second, rucking my boxers and my slacks down to my knees. I lay on my side, and fist my cock, paying special attention to the piercing at the tip of my penis. I look back at my phone screen, and see that Cady is already getting close, if her moans are anything to judge by.

She keeps dipping those two fingertips into her center, and then spreading her juices up to her clit. She moans loudly as she circles her clit. She's going to blow her stack in a second, unless I slow her down.

"Stop," I say.

Her eyes open, focusing on the screen. "What?"

"Get your vibrator out. Or… do you have a dildo?" I ask.

Her brow puckers. "I… I do…"

"Get them both," I say. "I'll wait. And I like this position, where I can see everything."

She bites her lip, but rolls away. I hear the drawer to her bedside table open, and a second later she reappears with a long, hard dildo made of the same dark pink plastic as her little vibrator.

She repositions herself, and looks at her phone. Uncertain, or maybe shy.

"Go ahead," I encourage. "I want to watch you come so hard that you can't see straight."

Cady turns the dildo on. I get the pleasure of watching as she takes it inside, her center so slick by now, her body so ready, that it goes in without much friction.

"Fuck!" she moans, wincing. "Oh, fuck, that's so good."

I keep my hand moving on my cock, squeezing a little more forcefully now. "Yeah? You like that?"

"Mmmhmmm," she nods.

"Use your vibrator on your clit," I say. "I want to see you come for me, princess."

She closes her eyes and turns it on, then applies the pink vibrator to her clit. "Ohhhh omigod…"

"Is it good?" I ask. I'm getting close now, my hand slamming up and down my cock like a jackhammer. "I want to hear it."

"Fuck, it's so good. I'm so close," she breathes. "Fuck, fuck…"

She comes, spasming around the dildo, peaking on a wordless cry. I only need two more pumps to be right there with her; my cock twitches and my balls draw up, and then I come all over my stomach.

I chuckle at Cady, who is carefully removing the pink dildo from her pussy. "That was... something."

She sets the dildo aside, and moves the camera so that I can see her face more. "That was hot."

"Yeah, it definitely was. There's nothing quite like watching your girlfriend lose herself like that. It gives me about ten ideas that I need to try out, ASAP."

She grins, but yawns. "When you get back, we can try all of them."

"Is that a promise?"

"It's a dare," she says, laughing. "I should go now, though. I made quite a mess over here."

"Alright. See you later."

After she hangs up, I get up too, cleaning myself up in the bathroom. Then I change into a bathrobe, laying down on the bed.

I called Cady my girlfriend, I think, laying back amongst the pillows. It's the first time I've said it out loud to her since the bridal shower, I think.

She didn't really react to it. That could mean that she is just rolling with the punches. She did say something about whatever you need to call me. I cringe, remembering that.

It could also mean that she likes it. She could love being the girlfriend, for all I know. It's hard to tell what she is thinking or feeling, honestly.

You could just ask her how she feels, I remind myself. *It's not that complicated.*

I rearrange the pillows under my head and grab my phone.

Hey. I just wanted to check and make sure that everything is good with you.

I shake my head and erase that. I try again.

Are you cool with me calling you my girlfriend?

Then I erase that too. She already said she was… didn't she? I don't want to make her second guess it.

I also don't want to be the one worrying about this shit. Maybe I should just take our relationship at face value. It's great sex, coupled with…

I sigh. Coupled with her desire to have a baby. I'm not directly against having kids. Hell, they are definitely part of my future, as far as I see it. But we're kind of putting the cart before the horse, having a baby together before we are really there yet.

Yeah, that part is kind of untouched, untalked about. And in order to talk about the other stuff, we'd have to address it.

So here I am, unable to formulate a text to say any of that. It's more of an in-person conversation, without a doubt. Shit, maybe a drunk conversation. At least that way we can both be honest with each other.

So instead of trying to feel Cady's level of commitment to our relationship out, I turn on the tv and zone out.

CADY

I sit in a Thai place around the corner from my house, fidgeting. It's the middle of the day on a Wednesday, and normally I would be at work. Instead, I'm straightening my white chiffon minidress, and fiddling with the table settings. I take a sip of my Thai iced tea, swallowing the sugary goodness.

I'm waiting for Jett, sitting here in a restaurant waiting, like any good wifey would do. Except I'm not his wife… I'm…

Is there even a word for what we are to each other? Probably not. Baby mama-to-be? Friend with benefits?

None of those are quite right. The term girlfriend isn't quite right either.

Girl who stopped drinking because a guy she likes doesn't love women who drink? Girl who will be dumped as soon as he realizes that he doesn't want a crazy, pregnant cow of a girlfriend? Yeah, those sound even worse.

Actually, it sounds pathetic. But after we talked about his judgy-ness about my drinking, I decided to lay off for a while. It's been a few weeks since I've had anything more than a glass of wine, and I feel okay about it.

Besides, there may be another good reason not to drink. I was counting the days since my last period yesterday, trying to do some math. It's totally possible that I'm just late; my cycle does do it's own thing a lot.

I decide not to worry about it for another week at the earliest. But yeah, not drinking is happening while I don't know, at least. If I do get my period, maybe I'll celebrate slash cry into a glass of wine.

There is one other thing I've realized, in the last few days. I like Jett. Like… really like him.

In fact, if I wasn't trying to get him to knock me up, right about now I would be confessing all my feelings to him. In a normal relationship, that is.

Too bad this was really the opposite of normal. I would just have to keep my feelings to myself, because a baby is more important to me right now than a potential love match.

…isn't it?

It's probably too late to decide, anyway, I think. *You're probably already fucking knocked up. And you should be glad that the choice is made, shouldn't you?*

I realize I'm nervous, and the thai tea probably isn't helping any. I push it away just as I spot him through the huge glass windows in the front. He looks ridiculously handsome, wearing a light grey suit and a starched white shirt underneath. His tattoos and his beard are on point, too. It's hard not to make a "hhhhuuuunnnnngghhhhhhh" noise when I look at him.

Yeah, it's only been a week since I've seen him. That doesn't stop me from wanting to rip open his shirt with my bare hands and nuzzle his bearded neck, right here in the restaurant. My cheeks color at the thought.

I must be hormonal, because I am honestly considering fucking him in the bathroom.

He looks for me, and I raise my hand. The grin that lights up his face when he sees me warms my insides. My lust shifts, turning to something sappier instead.

Stop it! I berate myself.

"Hey," he says. I stand up and embrace him. It's so fucking nice to be wrapped in his arms, to feel so small and so protected at once. I hide my face in between his broad chest and his muscular arm. He doesn't say anything about it, just chuckles.

"Hey," I say, my voice muffled by the wool of his suit jacket. I hug him hard for a second longer, battling with that unnamed squishy emotion.

Then I let him go, returning to my seat. He takes the seat across from me.

"I brought you something," he says, reaching into his jacket pocket. "It's little, don't worry."

"Oh yeah?" I say.

He pulls out a long white box, about six inches by nine, with a gold bow on top. Jett hands it over, and I pry it open. Inside I find an assortment of handmade chocolate truffles, each colorful and fancy. It comes with a card that has a picture of a cartoon dog shrugging. "For… you know, whatever…" the card reads.

"Amazing!" I say, laughing.

"Yeah, I saw the card, and I thought you would appreciate it," he says, his blue eyes sparkling.

"I do," I say, looking at the chocolates. "I know we're about to eat, but I can't resist. I have to try one."

I pick a truffle that's got a shiny green candy top, and take a bite. It's filled with a little pistachio ganache, and the sweet flavor makes my mouth water. "Omigod, it's so good."

"I'm glad you like it," Jett says, smiling. He picks up his menu. "Have you eaten here before?"

"Mmm, I have," I say, putting the top back on the chocolates. "I usually get their red curry bowl."

"That sounds good," he says, looking around for our waiter. He signals the young man, and orders two red curry bowls.

"I'm glad you're back," I say, trying to sound casual.

"Oh yeah?" he says, his brows raising. "You missed me, huh?"

"If I didn't make that clear enough over the last week, that's my bad." I give him a knowing look.

He leans forward, putting both of his elbows on the table.

"Yeah, I seem to remember something about how bad you wanted me to come back and give you—"

"Shh!" I say, shushing him.

"What? I was gonna say those chocolates." He grins at me, wicked as ever.

"Uh huh," I say, rolling my eyes.

"Is this thai tea?" he asks, pointing to my glass.

"It is! It's just too much sugar for me right now."

He takes the glass and takes a sip. "You weren't kidding. Why don't you get a glass of wine?"

"Because it's lunchtime?" I say, giving him an odd look. "And besides, I'm trying to cut back on drinking."

"What? Why? It's not because of that thing I said, is it?"

He looks genuinely concerned, which makes my heart twist in my chest.

"No," I assure him. "No, just... you know, preparing. I'm going to spend nine months not drinking, might as well get a head start."

He relaxes. "Oh. Alright. Oh, that reminds me, will you be my date to a wedding?"

"My not drinking makes you think of weddings?" I tease.

To my surprise, his cheeks color. "I just meant—"

"I'm kidding. Of course I'll go, if my schedule permits. Whose wedding is it?"

"It's a friend from college. Mason and Alex will be there too, and I'm pretty sure there will be some serious drinking involved."

"You are selling it by telling me how much drinking there will be?" I ask, squinting.

"Better than with my terrible friends," he says with a wink. "You've met them. They are fucking *terrible*."

I flap a hand. "When is it?"

"A couple of weekends from now."

"Alright. I'll just have to move some stuff around, I think."

Our food comes, and we laugh and chat through the meal. He tells a long story about his coworker Stuart, which is devastatingly funny. In the back of my mind though, there is a persistent little voice that will not shut up.

A little voice that asks questions I can't answer.

What if you're pregnant? Will you really just be done with him? Better yet, can you just be done?

If you're not pregnant, will you work up the nerve to ask him out? But that will put your plan off track, won't it?

Is it worth possibly sacrificing the ability to have a baby for... what, a shot at something real with a guy that you like?

"Hey," he says, his brow furrowing. "Are you okay? I feel like I lost you there."

"Oh, sorry," I say, shaking my head. I don't mean to lie, but it comes out of my mouth before I can stop it.

"Don't laugh, but I was wondering if Milo likes this new food I got him."

"So what you're saying is, cat food is far more interesting than my story." His eyes sparkle, letting me know he's kidding.

"Yes, exactly," I say, joking. "If you were looking for ways to make everything you say more interesting to me, that's where I would start.

"All right, noted." He eats a bite of curry and noodles.

"What are you going to wear? I'm trying to decide between a long light pink dress and a sort of red silk pantsuit," I say, pushing my bowl away.

Jett's eyes twinkle. "Wear the dress. I like the idea of you hitching it up around your waist when we sneak off to have sex during the reception."

"Jett!" I admonish. "That's not happening."

"It is!" he insists, looking pleased with himself. He pushes away his bowl. "You'll see."

"In your dreams." I roll my eyes.

"Every single time I close my eyes," he says with satisfaction. "That's less important than the more urgent question, though."

"Oh yeah?" I say. I take a sip of water. "And what's that?"

He drops his voice low. "Which of our offices has the more private parking deck? Because it's been a week since I've seen you naked. I can't go for another minute without running my hands all over—"

"Jett!" I whisper, looking around to see if anyone heard.

"What's that? You want me to get the check?" he says. He pulls out his wallet and drops a hundred dollar bill on the table. "Done."

"You can't seriously think that I'm going to have sex with you in the car." I frown at him.

"I do think so. Not only that, but you're going to scream my name when you come. I can tell that you need to get laid as badly as I do. That's why I think that we need a private corner of the parking deck to do it."

"Jett…" I say. He's totally serious now, as far as I can tell.

"You know what you need? You need to be told what to do, princess," he says, pushing his chair back and standing up. "Get your purse and get moving. If you hurry, I'll fuck you right away."

My eyes widen, and my whole body is suddenly hot. "And if I don't?"

Jett grins, coming around the table to lean in close to my ear. "I'll make you beg for it."

He slides his hand around the back of my neck, squeezing. It's a casually dominant gesture, and it makes me fucking weak in the knees. I feel my nipples stand at attention and my pussy get wet.

I let my head fall back, presenting my mouth to Jett for a kiss.

"Not yet," he says, his eyes steady on mine. "Get up and go to my car."

Trembling with anticipation, I rise, gathering my purse. Jett lets his hand drift down to the small of my back as we both leave the restaurant.

JETT

I eye Cady as we sit in the crowded church, mid-ceremony. She is wearing this floor-length dress made of light pink silky fabric, with roses all over the bodice. My fingers itch to touch the silky material. Actually, scratch that.

I want to touch *her*. The dress is just icing on the cake.

She notices me looking, and reaches out to take my hand. Squeezing my fingers a little, she gently nods towards the front of the church. I try to focus on the wedding at hand, adjusting myself on the hard pews.

The black-frocked minister drones on about the definition of marriage. I look at Mary and Danny, looking every bit like a wedding cake topper. Mary's expression is solemn, but Danny… he's actually dabbing at his eyes.

For some reason, seeing Danny nearly cry makes my eyes get misty. I look away, examining the church. It's small, only about sixty people are in attendance, all squashed into the pews together. The whole interior is done in white ash wood, and the ceiling ends in a wooden steeple.

I meditate on that for a while, counting the ceiling beams and imagining I am inside the ribcage of some great beast. I keep accidentally looking at Danny, and then looking at Cady to avoid looking at Danny.

I wonder if I'll ever be in Danny's place, I muse. Proposing to a girl, and walking down the aisle in front of everyone we know? That seems impossible.

I sneak a glance at Cady, who is tearing up now. I scoot closer and she leans against me, her tears falling onto my chest. There's probably going to be a wet spot on my black suit jacket, but it's okay. She feels so good right there, her body warm and just the right size for my embrace. I run my hand in little circles on her lower back, trying to soothe her.

I look ahead again, but this time I don't see Danny and Mary. This time, I imagine that Cady is walking down the aisle, wowing everyone with her perfectly fitted dress. I see myself in Danny's place, waiting for Cady at the end.

I imagine myself taking her trembling hand, and standing before the minister. We would say the words, he would pronounce us man and wife. I would pull her close, dipping her a little, and crush her lips against mine.

Suddenly, it no longer seems impossible. Instead, it seems… very doable.

Someday.

When everyone cheers and the bride and groom rush down the aisle, I finally snap out of it. Standing up, I stretch.

"Are you ready?" Cady asks. She stands up and gathers her purse.

"I'm game for anything that doesn't involve sitting on those pews," I say, exiting the row. I wait for Cady, and then we join the line of people who are slowly sauntering out of the church.

"It was a gorgeous service," she says. "Not that you would've noticed. I swear, every time I looked at you, you were either staring at me or looking up at the ceiling."

She elbows me playfully. I look down at her, dropping her hand in favor of slipping my arm around her waist.

"I did well for the first ten minutes of the ceremony. Then I was keeping to myself, staring at you, but you wouldn't let me leer."

Cady laughs. "How terrible of me. But what was I supposed to do, just let you sit there and think dirty thoughts? We're in a church, after all."

"I didn't know you were religious enough to care."

She rolls her eyes. "I'm not, but I was raised in a Catholic orphanage for a long time."

"Hmm," I say as we step out the church doors. It's dusk outside, and we follow the procession of people toward the banquet hall. "I didn't know you were raised Catholic."

"Hey, there is still tons and tons of stuff you don't know about me," she says, pulling a face. "Like, for instance... did you know that I went to an all-women's college."

"Wait, really?" I ask.

"Yes, really. I went to Agnes Scott College, right next door in Decatur. And then I went to Emory Law School."

"Hmm. I uh... I never went to college," I admit.

Her eyebrows shoot up. "Really?"

"Yep. You know what? I bet there are lots of things you don't know about me either."

We reach the banquet hall doors, and we stop and shake hands with Mary and Danny.

"Congratulations!" Cady says. "That was beautiful."

"It was," I affirm. Mary and Danny thank us, and we move inside.

The whole room is so elegant; cherry blossoms drip from the ceiling, and all the tables are elaborately decorated with tiny origami sculptures. The white-clad tables are set up throughout the room, with an area set aside for the band and for dancing.

"Wow," I say, impressed.

Cady bites her lip. "Let's look for our names on the table settings."

She takes my hand and weaves through the light crowd, looking at tiny place cards.

"I bet we're over there, by where Mason and Alex are awkwardly standing," I point out. The two of them look pretty slick, Alex in his grey suit and Mason in a navy one.

"Yep, I bet you're right." She smiles at me, heading over to them.

"Yo yo yo," Mason says, brightening. ""You guys looks amazing. Cady, there are no words for how breathtaking you are."

Cady blushes, her cheeks a shade darker than her lovely dress. "Thank you. You two look very dapper as well."

"Enough talk, let's find the bar," I suggest.

"Oh, there's a waiter circling with glasses of wine," Cady says, pointing.

"I don't think so," Alex intones. "I think the bar is over there. I'll make a bar run. What do you guys want?"

"Mmmm, whiskey and soda?" I say. I look to Cady. "What do you want?"

She shrugs a shoulder. "I'll snag a glass of wine from the waiter."

"I'll go with you to the bar," Mason says. He winks. "There's a cute girl bartending."

"Save it for her, champ," I say, rolling my eyes.

"Hah hah," Mason says, strolling off in the direction of the bar.

I turn to Cady. "You probably won't hear me say this often, but... let's get *drunk*."

I look for the waiter, and find that he's approaching.

"Why, just because it's a wedding?" Cady asks.

I pluck two glasses of red wine off of the waiter's tray, handing them to Cady. "Wait, hold on..."

I grab two more. The waiter couldn't care less, for which I'm thankful.

"Here," I say, to Cady. "To getting drunk, because it's a wedding."

She accepts my toast, clinking one of her wine glasses with mine. We both take a sip.

I make a face. This wine tastes cheap, like fake berries and stale water. Cady makes a similar expression.

"Ugh, this is awful," she says. "Maybe we got a bottle that was corked or something."

"Blugh," I say. "I grabbed all these glasses, so I feel like I kind of have to drink them."

"We'll make a game of it," Cady suggests. "What should we play?"

I think for a second. "Oh, how about Two Truths and a Lie? I tell you three facts about myself, and you have to guess which one is total bullshit. If you get it wrong, you drink!"

I grin triumphantly. She nods. "Alright. You start."

"Let's sit down while I think of which ones to start with," I say. I scope out our place cards, and sit in an uncomfortable metal chair. I set my wine glasses down, and watch Cady do the same. "This chair leaves something to be desired."

"Shhh," Cady says, her eyes twinkling. "Wait until we leave to complain."

"Okay. Alright, are you ready?" I ask.

"Always," she fires back.

I grin. "Alright. Number one. I was completely and entirely obsessed with Babe Ruth as a kid."

She looks thoughtful. "Hmmm. I mean, you did grow to play major league baseball for a few years."

"I did! Ummm…. number two. The worst job I ever had was at Taco Bell as a teenager. I worked on the food line."

"Can't tell," she says, shaking her head. "This would be a lot easier if you were a terrible liar."

"Hey, maybe I am!" I say. "You don't know."

"No, I don't." She sighs dramatically.

"Last one. Number three. I have been to Machu Picchu, *twice*."

"Whhhhattttt," she says. "How am I supposed to choose?"

"Very carefully," I recommend. "Which one do you think is the lie?"

"Mmmm… maybe the one about Machu Picchu?" she guesses.

"Nope," I say with a grin. "I have, in fact, been there twice."

Cady takes the smallest sip of her wine. "Okay. Then it's got to be the Taco Bell thing?"

"Incorrect! I did actually work at Taco Bell for a summer. That job sucked."

She gapes for a second. "So you didn't care about baseball when you were little?"

"I did, but not Babe Ruth. I was all about Ken Griffey Jr. I had all his stats memorized." I sip from my wine. "All right…"

"Ladies and gentlemen," the lead singer of the wedding band cuts in over a microphone. "You have about fifteen minutes of mingling before we introduce the bride and groom for their first dance."

I wiggle my eyebrows at Cady. "Perfect. Just the amount of time I need to guess which of your facts is a lie."

"Okay," she says, thinking. "Oh! Number one. I've never been out of the continental U.S."

I screw up my face. "That can't be true. Can it?"

"I don't know, you tell me. Second — I have a collection of tiny sweaters for Milo."

"Well, I know that has to be true," I laugh.

"Yeah, yeah. Alright, the third one is the charm. I wanted to be a grocery bagger when I was a kid."

"A grocery bagger?" I say, wrinkling my nose. "I think that's the lie."

"Haha!" she says. "No. I went through a phase were I thought that grocery bagging was the bee's knees."

"So… you haven't been outside the U.S.? Not even to Hawaii?" I say, cocking my head.

"That's true. Until I was twenty five, I had never left the state of Georgia."

I shake my head. "That seems impossible. I honestly would never have thought you were untravelled. I've been everywhere, except the whole Indian subcontinent."

"This is fun," she says, sitting back in her seat. "I like this game a lot."

"Okay. Let's go again," I say, sipping the wine. "One — I hate spiders. Two — I'm crazy good at water skiing. Three — I've been in a weird competition with Jax for years, over who is the taller one. It involves us sending each other selfies while next to abnormally small things, like miniature ponies."

"Hmm," she says, squinting. "Interesting. I'm going to go with…. the spider thing?"

"Yes!" I grin. "Does that mean I drink?"

"Yes it does. In the very strict rules of this game that you definitely did not make up." She raises her wine glass to me, and I clink mine against hers.

I take a couple long swallows, letting the wine slide down my throat.

"Definitely not made up," I say. "Now you go."

"Okay, let's see. Uhhhh… one, I got offered a promotion at work recently."

"You did?" I ask.

"I don't know, did I?" she says coyly. "Two — in middle school, I was OBSESSED with Leonardo diCaprio. I would lie in bed at night, wondering when — not if — we would meet."

I raise my eyebrows. "That's a little too believable."

She cracks up. "You are impossible to play this game with."

"I'll stop, I swear. What's the third fact?"

"I love all eighties music. Michael Jackson, Steely Dan, a-ha, Van Halen… I could listen to that all day."

"I'm going to go all in on the odds that number two is the lie," I guess.

Cady shakes her head. "Nope. I had Leo's name written everywhere that I could doodle. I was really convinced that we were meant to be."

"What?" I say. I take a gulp of my wine, finishing the glass. "Okay… then… eighties music?"

"Yep!" she says, triumphant. "I hate most eighties music. Obviously there are exceptions, but… yeah. It mostly makes me want to rip my ears off."

"Descriptive! But I think you'd look weird without your ears."

"Then you'd be stuck trying to explain to people that I ripped my own ears off. I would be deaf, in this scenario."

"You have a strange imagination," I say. "Come on, the wine isn't that bad, is it? You've hardly drank any."

She opens her mouth, but she's cut off.

"Alright, everyone," the lead singer says into the microphone. "It's my pleasure to introduce to you all Mr. and Mrs. Burns! They're going to be doing their first dance now."

The band starts playing their own cover of Bonnie Raitt's "Something To Talk About", and Danny leads Mary out onto the dance floor. As I watch, Danny takes Mary in his arms and starts to slow dance. They grin at each other, and Mary whispers something.

Whatever Mary says, it makes Danny cup her face and kiss her.

"Awww," Cady sighs beside me. "They really, really love each other."

The band transitions to playing an older Sade song. The singer announces, "Everyone is invited to dance with the new couple!"

I stand up, offering Cady my hand. She glances at me, then laughs. "Oh, are we doing this now?"

"We are."

She puts her hand in mine, and I tug her to her feet. Leading the way to the dance floor, I pull her into my arms, settling into a comfortable cadence. Chest to chest, hips pressed to hips, we sway.

Cady lays her head against my chest. I hold her hand in mine, my other arm around her waist. I feel lucky to be holding her, lucky to have met her on that rooftop at all.

My chest feels suddenly tight, like my chest can't possibly contain all of my emotions. They're too big and too bright for the space.

I love her, I realize. *This is what love feels like.*

The question remains, how do I tell her?

CADY

"Jett," I whisper. "Are you awake?"

I'm checking to make sure that Jett is definitely asleep. He's sprawled out like a king in my bed, his mouth open a little. I move around a bit, but it appears he's out.

That's good, because I am feeling super nauseated... and I think I know why.

Getting up, I duck into my walk-in closet and put on my robe. Sneaking into my bathroom, I close the door as quietly as possible, then turn on the light. I go to the toilet and crouch down, my mouth filling with saliva.

Without any further warning, I suddenly start vomiting. I try to be quiet as I throw up all the food I ate for dinner, my eyes watering. When I am out of food, I dry heave for a while, producing nothing but bile.

At length, I sit back on the floor in the space between the toilet and the sink. I grab a bit of toilet paper and close my eyes, wiping at my mouth. I'm still super nauseated, but nothing more seems to want to come up.

I'm willing to bet that I didn't just happen to eat something bad. I think I'm pregnant, just like I wanted. Except now I'm extremely stressed about the possibility of being knocked up.

It's just... too soon. I never thought I would feel this way, especially not when I cried in my car after that doctor's appointment.

But here I am. After a bit, I stand up on shaky legs. I go to the sink, biting my lip as I open the cabinet below, pulling out a small brown paper bag.

I hesitate, then lock the bathroom door. Upending the brown paper bag, I empty the contents into the sink.

Three different brands of pregnancy tests stare back at me. I pick up the first one, my fingers trembling a little. I read the instructions thoroughly, then open the box. I peel away the cellophane wrapper on the stick.

Glancing up at my reflection in the mirror, I steel myself.

You won't gain anything by not taking the test, I warn myself. Just do it. It's better to know.

Taking a deep breath, I take the stick with me to the toilet. After a minute, I am able to actually pee, and I make sure to saturate the stick.

I flush, then set the stick on the counter. I only have to wait two to three minutes. I can do that.

I wash my hands, then try to find a comfortable standing position in the bathroom. I refuse to simply stand over the stick, staring down at it. So I keep shifting positions, crossing and uncrossing my arms while I wait impatiently.

This is it, I tell myself. *If the test is positive, you have to make a decision. Either tell Jett your feelings and risk losing him and being rejected... or tell him you're through, even though that might be the worst decision possible.*

Focusing on my breathing, I close my eyes. The idea of

never seeing Jett again... of waking up alone. It's almost too much to bear. I tear up at the thought of Jett leaving my apartment, never to return.

The scary thing is, that could be the outcome either way. Either because I'm brave enough to say what's in my heart, or because I'm too chickenshit to explain why I can't continue to see him.

I take a deep breath and open my eyes. Looking down at the stick, my stomach does flips.

It's positive.

I'm pregnant.

Never in my life have I been so damned giddy and yet so desperately depressed at once.

This, this baby, is what I wanted. What I worked for. The reason I sought Jett out in the first place. I press my hands against my perfectly flat abdomen and look at myself in the mirror.

A woman looks back at me, clad in her robe, dark hair streaming around her face.

She's a stranger.

She's a mother.

Someone who isn't alone.

I've *always* been alone.

I cup my hands over my face, my tears overflowing. I'm crying tears of joy, but there are tears of anguish, too. I feel like I'm gaining a baby, which is amazing... but I'm suddenly wholly certain that I am going to lose Jett.

I wrap my arms around myself, imagining the many ways that the conversation I don't want to have will go. Tears stream down my face as I picture it. Me going out there and telling him that I'm pregnant... and I have all these *feelings* for him, too.

I also imagine it going the opposite way. I tell him that I can't see him anymore, and refuse to explain why.

Both ways make my heart twist in my chest. Both ways have an equal chance of Jett walking out on me, right here and now.

I see myself in the mirror, my shoulders hunched, my tears making my mascara run. I force myself to take slow, deliberate breaths. Wiping at my eyes, I use a big handful of toilet paper to remove the worst of the mascara from around my eyes.

Remember, this is positive news. You both knew this was coming. You told him from the start that this is what you wanted.

I tidy up the tests, throwing away the used one. My nausea has disappeared, gone as soon as I found out I am pregnant.

I square my shoulders, turning off the bathroom light as I leave. I pad back to the bedroom, the moonlight coming from the window throwing stripes across Jett. I push back the covers, hesitating.

Do I curl up with Jett and pretend nothing happened?

Part of me says yes. Part of me wants nothing more than to let Jett spoon me, drifting off to sleep peacefully.

Jett stirs. His voice is pure gravel. "You okay?"

I can't help the tears that spring forward. "No. No, I'm not."

He sits up, befuddled and sleepy.

"What's wrong?" he asks, taking one of my hands.

I take a deep breath. It's now or never, I figure.

"I just took a pregnancy test," I say, my voice shaking.

"Uhhh... okay..." He looks more confused than before.

"I'm pregnant," I admit, sniffling.

He goes stiff as a board. "Oh. Oh, fuck. Really?"

"Yeah. You're going to be a daddy," I say, barely able to rein in my tears.

He looks at my flat stomach, and grazes it with the back of his knuckles. "I can't believe we made a person."

"Well, it's just a mass of cells at the moment." I reach for his hand, but he pulls away.

Oh god, it's already happening. With those two words, *I'm pregnant*, I made myself unattractive.

Jett glances at my petrified face and takes my hand.

"I'm sorry, I just wasn't expecting you to say that," he says, shaking his head. "Congratulations, of course."

I feel disappointment coming off of him in waves, and I panic. What can I say that will relieve both of us of any obligation to one another?

"I might be moving to Seattle!" I blurt out.

"You... *what?*" he asks. His tone goes completely harsh, and he drops my hand. "When were you planning to tell me? I am your boyfriend, you know. Or is that over, now that you've gotten what you wanted?"

"What?" I say, recoiling. That isn't what I meant, not in the least. How could he have misunderstood my intentions so... *wildly?*

"You heard me," he says, moving to the edge of the bed. He reaches down for his boxer briefs, and gets them on.

"I'm just..." I say, at a loss. I want to back up, to take back my statement, but I didn't really do anything wrong. I just told him the truth. "I don't know that I'm moving to Seattle, but it is possible. It's just an offer that I got. I'm trying to figure things out. And I just found out that I'm pregnant less than ten minutes ago!"

He puts on his pants. "I am really happy for you. I am. But... you're moving across the country, now that you found out?"

"The two things have nothing to do with one another." I cross my arms, disgruntled.

He scowls at me, and picks his shirt up.

"Right. You just happened to tell me both of them at one time?" He puts his shirt on, not bothering to button it. "You know, when Jax called you a people-user, I got mad at him. But maybe he was right."

"He said *what?*" I say, my voice rising. This is spiraling out of control, and fast.

"I'm saying, maybe he finally got *something* right. You got what you needed out of me, and now you're ready to run."

"Okay, everything you're saying sounds super dramatic," I accuse. "Besides, it's hardly your decision what I do with my body and *my* baby. You signed away your parental rights, buddy."

I see him freeze, his whole body clenching. He looks at the floor for a moment.

Jett turns toward me, a nasty expression on his face. "If I don't leave now, I'm going to say something I regret."

"So leave!" I say, throwing my hands up in the air. "No one is stopping you. There's the door."

This seems to incense him.

"If I leave, I'm not coming back," he warns.

Not one to take in idle threat lying down, I shout, "Good! Go!"

He hesitates for just a beat, then storms out of the bedroom. A few seconds later, I hear the front door slam.

He's gone, just like that.

And me? I'm absolutely gutted, shaking with the force of my anger and my anguish. I didn't know that I had that inside me, to blow up at someone like that. Jett just pulled it out of me, somehow.

Tears leak down my face, and I wipe them away roughly. I look at the door, somehow expecting Jett to return, to come back through that door and say he's sorry.

But after a minute, it becomes apparent that he's really, truly not coming back.

I throw myself onto the bed face first, wondering what the fuck just happened. Did we break up? Did we just have an argument? I wish I knew.

He seemed really really angry when I said I might be moving. And before that... he was, what? Disappointed?

I replay the scene again and again, trying to find a clue as to what happened.

But there is nothing. I roll over and look at what I think of as his side of the bed. It's empty, completely desolate.

Just like I imagined in the bathroom. Have I created a self-fulfilling prophecy?

I lie in bed, my tears staining the pillow. Then another bout of nausea hits, and I'm too busy scrambling to make it to the bathroom to think about it anymore.

JETT

Driving home in the middle of the night, I am furious.

At myself, for throwing down an ultimatum during an argument.

But mostly at her, for so many things.

I'd imagined that moment in my mind, I guess. The time when she tells me she's pregnant, and then throws herself in my arms. In my mind, some grand confession of love would follow, with both of us in tears.

Except, it didn't happen that way at all.

It started simply. Something is wrong with Cady, I can just tell.

"You okay?" I ask, barely opening my eyes.

She's sitting on the edge of the bed, wearing her white bathrobe, and looking tearful.

"No. No, I'm not," she admits, her voice cracking a little.

I sit up, just to get my blood pumping to my brain.

"What's wrong?" I ask, still mostly asleep.

Cady looks at me. Her expression says that a storm is brewing, but she's holding it back a bit.

"I just took a pregnancy test," she announces.

"Uhhh… okay…" I try to wait for her to finish, because I feel like the other shoe is waiting to drop.

She sniffs and wipes at her eye. "I'm pregnant."

I stiffen. It's happening now, like really happening. She's pregnant, and we both have so much to say. My mind is working overtime, struggling to comprehend. "Oh. Oh, fuck. Really?"

"Yeah. You're going to be a daddy," she says, emotion making her voice thick.

I don't know what to do, so I look at her belly. It seems impossible that right this very second, there is a baby with half my DNA growing inside there. I reach out and touch her stomach. "I can't believe we made a person."

"Well, it's just a mass of cells at the moment." She swats at my hand, and I move away. It must be a lot, learning that your body is going to be occupied by another living being. I respect that.

I glance up at her and catch her face, reading the anxiety there. Fuck it, if she's afraid, I'm going to try to comfort her. I take her hand and squeeze it.

"I'm sorry, I just wasn't expecting you to say that," I say, shaking my head. "Congratulations, of course."

When she doesn't say anything, I start to worry. What if she doesn't want to hear my intended heartfelt declarations? What if she doesn't ever want to hear them, period?

"I might be moving to Seattle!" she blurts.

That was… not what I wanted to hear.

"You… *what?*" I demand. I let go of her hand. "When were you planning to tell me? I am your boyfriend, you know. Or is that over, now that you've gotten what you wanted?"

"What?" she asks. She is visibly uncomfortable with what I am saying.

"You heard me," I say. I moving to the opposite edge of the bed. I can"t have this conversation naked, so I reach down for my underwear and stand up to pull them on.

"I'm just… I don't know that I'm moving to Seattle, but it is possible. It's just an offer that I got. I'm trying to figure things out. And I just found out that I'm pregnant less than ten minutes ago!"

What in the fuck? I'm so confused. I find my pants, and pull them on.

"I am really happy for you. I am. But… you're moving across the country, now that you found out?"

"The two things have nothing to do with one another." She crosses her arms.

"Right. You just happened to tell me both of them at one time?"

I pull my shirt on, steaming. I can't remember being this mad at a woman, ever. How does she not see that one has everything to do with the other? I hear Jax's voice, in the back of my mind. *I told you so.*

"You know, when Jax called you a people-user, I got mad at him. But maybe he was right."

"He said *what?*" Her voice goes up an octave.

"I'm saying, maybe he finally got *something* right. You got what you needed out of me, and now you're ready to run."

"Okay, everything you're saying sounds super dramatic," she spits at me. "Besides, it's hardly your decision what I do with my body and *my* baby. You signed away your parental rights, buddy."

I stop, going cold. It's only existed for ten minutes, and yet she's already telling me that I don't have any right to my child? Jesus fucking christ. How is this fair?

I turn toward her, trying to control my growing rage. I need to leave, before I snap. "If I don't leave now, I'm going to say something I regret."

"So leave!" she shouts, throwing her hands up. "No one is stopping you. There's the door."

I start to see red. No one has ever worked me up so much.

"If I leave, I'm not coming back," I yell at her. I don't mean it really, but it feels good to say.

Her face falls into a grim expression. "Good! Go!"

I hesitate for a second. This is really our first fight... but honestly? The way she sounds makes me think that it might also be our last.

I turn away from her and stomp out of the apartment, so mad I can barely see straight. When I get to the car, I sit with the engine running for a few minutes. I need to calm down before I drive, because I feel like I might run anybody that looks at me wrong right off the road.

I make it home okay, but when I get to bed, sleep eludes me for ages. I roll over and try not to spend the entire remainder of the night replaying and replaying the same scene.

When I finally do sleep, it is plagued with dreams. In them, Cady is a 50s housewife in a typical 50s ranch house, sort of like the neighborhood in Edward Scissorhands. Cady is massively pregnant, she's busy packing her suitcase.

"We talked about this!" she says, smiling. "I have to move to Seattle! It's not personal, I just don't love you!"

And there I am, naked for some reason, looking on as she packs her bag.

I wake with a start, bile filling my mouth. Groaning at the sunlight and the birds chirping, I head to shower. When I get to the bathroom, though, I stop. There next to the sink is Cady's toothbrush, her only concession to my insistence that girlfriends leave things at their boyfriend's places.

I hurry through my shower routine, rushing to get dressed. But then when I'm dressed, I stop.

Where am I about to go? I wonder. For the first day in a long time, I don't feel like working out.

Actually, I haven't felt so dissatisfied since Emily broke up with me. I wonder if Cady sensed the same wrongness in me that Emily did? Maybe that was why she dropped the Seattle bomb at the same time she told me she was pregnant.

I sit back down on my bed. *Cady is pregnant. We made a life, together.*

I crack my knuckles. The thought of my DNA becoming a *person* terrifies me and yet elates me. I imagine if it is a boy, he'll look just like me. Cady was right when she said that family resemblance is strong in the James clan.

If it's a little girl, though…

My heart squeezes uncomfortably. If Cady has a little girl, she'll look just like Cady. I imagine Cady bouncing the baby in her arms and cooing.

I clench my fists. What if the whole fight last night was Cady's way of letting me down gently, though? What do I do if she just doesn't want to be with me and moving to Seattle is just a convenient excuse to get out of the relationship?

I find my phone and text Mason and Alex.

I need to go do something ASAP. I have to get out of my head.

Less than a minute later, Alex responds.

Want to go for a hike? I'm gearing up to hike up near Stone Mountain soon.

Mason joins in. *I'm down to hike.*

I respond, *I'll get ready. Meet at Alex's house?*
I head to my closet to get ready.

CADY

My phone chirps, and I jump out of my seat to grab it. It's just another work email, though. I feel disappointment down to my bones.

I sigh and sit my pajama-wearing butt back on the couch. I am officially taking a whole day off of work to pout and watch bad reality TV while I try to figure out my life. Also, I spent most of my early morning throwing up, so I'm feeling more than a little fragile right now.

So far, I've texted Olive a frowny face and stared at the contents of my fridge, trying to imagine eating something. Putting Real Housewives on the TV is the third task I've assigned myself, and that is going well.

By well, I mean that I am slumped over, distractedly watching TV and jumping up anytime my phone makes a noise. It chirps again, and I see it's a text from Olive.

Sorry I'm so late answering this... I've been really tied up at Johann's house.

I roll my eyes at the reference to all the kinky sex she's having. I get it, Olive, you're banging some really hot

European dude with strange tastes. I think about what to say in response.

Jett and I had a really, really big fight. We might have broken up.

Wait, you don't know whether you ended things?

Can you just come over? I have a couple of things to catch you up on.

Be there soon. Stopping for pastries and coffee.

...make mine a decaf.

😱😱😱😱*!!! Are you sure??? I have so many questions!!*

I put my phone down and look askance at the TV. A blonde woman is arguing with a brunette, screaming something about not ever going after her husband. I legitimately have no idea what they are fighting about, and I don't really care.

Milo appears, demanding attention, and I scoop him up. I hold him on my lap, and Milo purrs and kneads my heavy sweatpants.

I realize that Milo is going to be a big brother, and I well up.

"Are you going to be a good big brother?" I ask him, wiping away the tears that cling to my eyelashes. "Damn hormones, making me cry at everything."

I know it's not just the hormones, though. It's Jett and this stupid fight that we had.

He called me a people user, though.

"Am I a people user?" I ask aloud.

Milo seems unaffected by my emotional state as he butts his head against my hand, seeking more affection. I stroke his silky head and stare into his big bright blue eyes.

"Milo, what am I doing?" I ask. "Am I crazy to be trying to have a relationship with the guy that was just supposed to knock me up?"

I bite my lip. The thing is, I have gone past trying to have a relationship. I've tumbled head first into *I think I'm in love with you* territory, and I'm fast approaching *I need you in my life* world.

A little part of me demands to know if Jett is as miserable as I am. *He's probably not crying*, I admit to myself. *He's probably relieved. I just set him free.*

That's not fair, though. I pick up my phone and check Jett's texts, hoping against hope that there will be something new. But no, the same texts are there from last night.

I exhale, feeling like an emotional teenager. It just isn't fair that I should have to worry and wonder how he feels.

In a perfect world, I would just magically know how Jett feels, on a scale of one to ten. But what would that do, exactly? One will send me running to Seattle as fast as I can; I don't know what ten would do, honestly.

The door buzzes, and I get up to answer it. A little part of me secretly hopes to see Jett standing there, looking tall and dangerous.

But when I look, it's just Olive. I press the button to buzz her up and unlock the door, then return to the couch. Olive knocks, then opens the door.

She looks fabulous as always, wearing a gorgeous grey silk dress, her hair twisted into a neat chignon.

"Hey, buddy," she says, assessing my situation. She holds up a coffee carrier in one hand and a pastry bag in the other. "I brought food."

For some reason, that makes me tear up again.

"Thanks. You're a really good friend." I sniffle. "And you look really cute."

Olive comes over to the couch. "Scootch."

I move over, and she hands me the coffees in their brown paper carrier. She sits, elegant even now.

"So?" she prompts. "Start with the biggest news."

I take a deep breath, and she pulls the coffee carrier

out of my hand and frees both of the paper cups. She hands mine to me.

"Wellllll...." I say. "As of eight hours ago, I'm pregnant."

"Yayyyy!" Olive says, leaning over and hugging me. "I figured that was the case. I'm so happy for you! And for your baby, because he or she is going to have the best mom and aunt ever."

"I know. I should be happy," I say, sitting back. "But when I told Jett, it wasn't exactly a joyous event."

"Tell me everything." Olive opens the pastry bag and hands me a blackberry danish.

I accept it with a sigh. "I told him, and he just sort of looked dazed. He eventually congratulated me, but it generally wasn't a very happy moment."

"And you had an argument about that?" Olive asks, cocking her head.

"No. We had an argument because I told him I might be moving for this promotion, and he called me a people user."

Her mouth drops into an O. "What? Wait wait wait, back up. What promotion?"

I bite my lip. "You can't tell anyone at work, but the company is expanding. I've been offered a job opening the litigation branch in Seattle."

I legitimately think that Olive is going to explode with happiness.

"Me too!!" she says. "They asked me not to tell anyone at work, though!"

"Really?" I say. "Oh, thank god. I don't know how I would have made it in Seattle without you!"

"Wait, but..." Olive looks a little confused. "What about Jett?"

"Right. I wasn't very smooth about it. I just blurted

that fact out, because I felt like he was really disappointed at my other news. I wanted to let him know that I don't absolutely need him to do anything. I figured I've lived alone before…"

"What? Why would you tell him you don't need him?" she asks, baffled.

"Well, I don't," I answer.

"You're right, you will live… but you wouldn't drive him away, right?"

"Right. I mean… we never really got to talk about that, because of the argument."

"When did this happen?"

"Oh, in the middle of the freaking night."

Olive eyes me. "Let me get this straight. You are stupid in love with this guy, who happens to have been trying to knock you up."

"I—"

"Let me finish," she says sternly. "Instead of saying that, you woke him up—"

"I didn't wake him up on purpose though—"

She swats my arm. "You woke him in the middle of the night to say that you were pregnant. No talk of feelings, just cold hard facts. Then you were surprised when he didn't respond how you wanted him to?"

"He told me that I was a people user," I say stubbornly.

"What was the context, though? That's the point I'm trying to make here."

I sip my coffee to give myself some time to think. "I said I was moving to Seattle. He asked when I was planning to tell him. And then he implied that I've been using him for his sperm."

Olive gives me this no DUH face. "Cady, I swear, you are so damn thick sometimes. He obviously feels strongly about you, and was probably really put off by your take no prisoners attitude."

"I was just trying to give him an out," I protest weakly.

Olive sets down her pastry and pats my arm.

"I know that we don't normally talk about this, but... I think you are treating him as if he was your family. Like, you see it as giving him a free pass to walk away... but I don't think he sees it that way. I mean, I could be wrong, but... I don't think I am."

"So you're saying... what?"

"Tell him how you feel, dummy," Olive says.

"But—"

"No buts! If you're going to be devastated, at least make sure it's not the result of a miscommunication." She picks up her danish and takes a huge bite. She mmmmms at the taste of it, crumbs all over her mouth.

"I don't know..." I say, setting my danish aside.

She swallows for a second. "Seriously? Don't be stupid. You're obviously in love with him. He is probably in love with you... there is literally no reason not to just *say* something."

I gather my hair with my free hand, tugging on it. "You think so?"

"I'm going to put all of *this*," she gestures to me. "Down to pregnancy hormones. You have never been so indecisive, ever."

"If what you say is true, and Jett feels... whatever he feels for me," I say. "Then why didn't he just say so?"

"The same reason you didn't tell him you love him. You guys are both chicken shit." Olive sighs. "I'm sure that he is damaged in some way, just like you. Otherwise you wouldn't even like... find him attractive."

"Oh, I don't know. Have you seen him? He's tall, handsome, and tattooed."

Olive cracks a smile. "I have seen him. I didn't mean to imply that he's physically unattractive, he's obviously a dream boat. It's just… it's important that your insides match as well as your outsides."

I sigh. "Well, if you mean that we both have damage from our shitty childhoods, you're right."

She puts her arm around me. "Listen. You're going to get through this. You have me on your side, no matter what. You have the promotion. You have the baby."

"Yeah, but… what if I don't have Jett?" I say, tearing up again.

"Well, you won't know until you talk to him properly." She shrugs. "I think that's all you can do."

"Ughhhhh, you're right. I have to talk to him." I suddenly feel thirsty.

I get up, and see spots before my eyes. Everything is fuzzy and hazy.

That's the last memory I have before I black out.

JETT

I'm hiking uphill at full steam, a dozen yards ahead of Mason and Alex. There's nothing to focus on but my breathing and the trees on either side of the trail, and I kind of like it that way. It's peaceful here, just the dark brown and vivid green of the foliage, the dark brown clay underfoot as I climb.

If I go hard enough, I can't think about Cady. So that's nice, I guess.

Eventually I realize that I've left Alex and Mason behind, so I slow down and wait for them. I find a tree and lean against it, breathing hard.

A few minutes later, the guys come up the path.

"I was wondering if we would ever see you again, or if you would just keep rocketing to outer space," Alex jokes.

I push off of the tree. "Yeah, sorry about that. I am just really worked up."

Mason takes a sip of his water. "You said that you and Cady had a fight. What was it about?"

"She's pregnant," I say, scrunching my face up.

"It was my understanding that that was the goal," Alex says.

"Right. She told me in the middle of the night, and then she said she might move to Seattle." I start walking uphill again, and my friends follow me.

"Whoa, what?" Mason asks. "I assume that she realizes that's across the whole damn country?"

"Yeah, I think so," I say, shaking my head.

Alex looks at me. "How do you feel about her maybe leaving?"

"Honestly? I fucking hate the idea of Cady and my unborn child leaving. I kind of get the sense that if they go, I won't see them again."

"You think she would do that?" Alex says, his brow furrowing.

"I don't know. I'm trying to wrap my head around what she might do or think," I say.

We reach the tree line, and emerge from the woods. I look around; the reddish-brown clay has receded, leaving only the bare dark grey stone underfoot.

Here and there, clumps of shrubbery grow in little nooks and crannies, but otherwise there's nothing before us but a climbing dome of rock. The bare stone is streaked with lime, marking wide swaths light green-blue.

We've reached the summit, where we can't go further without doing some serious rock climbing.

"Fuck," I say, turning to the guys. "What now?"

"We should rest a little," Mason suggests. "Then we can go back down."

I squint as I look around. "How about over there, on that rock formation? It kind of looks like a bench."

"Sounds good," Alex says, leading the way.

Alex and Mason sit down, but I can't be still, even for such a small space of time. I stretch my quads out instead.

"You are wired," Mason observes. "What are you going to do?"

"About Cady?"

He nods.

"I don't know, man."

"You can't let her go without talking to her," Alex says. "It's as simple as that."

"And what am I going to say, exactly?"

"Say what you feel," Mason suggests.

"Yeah, but what if what I feel is… complicated?"

"Like what?" Mason asks, crossing his arms.

I look off into the distance. "I just feel like… I embarked on this whole adventure because I thought she was hot… and then I started to actually like her. And just when I thought that I felt more for her, she started to pull back. Then she drops this bomb on me…"

"The fact that she's going to Seattle, or the pregnancy?" Alex asks.

"Both of them!" I say, throwing my arms up in the air.

"Do you think that maybe she's trying to give you an out by bringing up the whole Seattle thing?" Mason says, looking speculative.

"Why would she do that?" I ask.

"Because you clearly haven't talked about your feelings," he shrugs. "Otherwise, we wouldn't be here right now, trying to figure things out."

"Yeah. It would all be a lot easier if you and Cady just talked really frankly," Alex adds.

I look around for a second, trying to get my bearings.

"Should we head back down?" I ask.

"Seriously, dude?" Mason says, shaking his head. "No, we're not going back down until you face facts. You made a lot of progress as a person after Emily left, but at the first sign of trouble with Cady, you're going to bail?"

"Yeah," Alex says, nodding emphatically. "You need to figure out what the worst thing is that can happen."

I cross my arms. "The worst thing? Cady decides that she doesn't want me. Or... actually, the worst thing is that Jax was right, and Cady's a people user, just like my mom. I don't want to chase Cady around the country and continue that cycle."

That throws Mason and Alex for a loop.

"That is dark," Mason says. "I think... I think the only thing you can do is be honest with her."

"He's right," Alex says. "If things aren't going how you had hoped, I think the next step is to figure out how you want them to go."

I rub the back of my neck. "Ideally?"

"Yeah, assuming everything goes perfectly," Alex answers.

I think about it for a second. "I mean, ideally Cady stays put. She doesn't move to Seattle, and we... like, raise the baby together."

Mason grins. "That's your ideal scenario?"

"Yeah. If I'm honest."

Mason looks at Alex. "I think Jett's in love."

I get defensive. "So? So what?"

"Mason is just being immature. What he should have said is that you should tell her that you love her, man. That's the only way to know her feelings for sure. Just... admit your own," Alex says.

"Yeah, what he said." Mason looks pleased.

"Yeah, but what if—" I start.

"Nope!" Alex says. "No more of this. You're a grown-ass man. Go show Cady that you have a backbone made of steel. In fact, call her right now."

"Can't. I left my phone in the car," I shrug.

"Well, now would be an appropriate time to insist that

we head back down, then," Mason says. He and Alex stand up. "Come on, let's race to the bottom."

He tears off down the trail. Alex looks at me for a beat, then follows suit. I have no choice but to head down the trail after them, picking up speed as I go.

Although the way down is much easier and faster than the way up was, I am glad for the fifteen minutes of silence. I need to psych myself up if I'm going to talk to Cady.

If I'm going to be open and truthful with her, I have a lot to say.

Or… not a lot, actually. I just have to say the three magic words.

I love you.

Preferably I will demand that she stays here in Atlanta… and she will simper.

Yeah, right, I think. Alright, so no simpering. It's not Cady's bag. Her strength is actually one of the things I like most about her.

And then… the rest is up to her. I swallow as I lope down the trail after my friends, my muscles burning.

When we get back to Alex's Suburban, the first thing I do is check my phone. Not that I will say what I have to say over the phone, but maybe Cady has called me in the past hour an a half.

When I check my phone, I see three missed calls from a number I don't recognize. We hop in the car and head back into the city, and I check the lone voicemail that came from the number I don't know.

I open a bottle of water and chug most of it down as I listen.

"Hey Jett," a familiar sounding woman says. "It's Olive, Cady's friend. Cady and I are heading to Peachtree General right now…"

I do an honest to god spit take.

"She passed out at her apartment. I just thought maybe you would want to know that she's there? Call me if you want…"

I hang up and look up at Mason, who is watching me with concern.

"We have to get to Peachtree General. Something happened to Cady," I say, starting to tremble.

Alex glances at me in the rearview mirror, then presses on the gas. "Alright. I hope everyone is wearing a seat belt…"

As the scenery outside my window starts to whiz by, I dial Olive's number, praying.

Please let Cady be okay.

CADY

I am in the emergency room, laying on the hospital bed, and I am embarrassed. I sigh heavily, and crane my neck to try to see around the big green hospital curtains that have been pulled for my privacy.

I look down at my right arm, wishing that I could scratch the sterile tape that holds my IV in place. Instead, I make do with scratching the skin right next to it, but it's not very satisfying. I grunt at the tape.

"I'm sorry that they're keeping you for observation tonight," Olive says, for probably the tenth time. "I just freaked out when you fainted."

"It's okay," I say, shrugging. "Better safe than sorry. Besides, with this IV, I should be super hydrated. Who knew that a little vomiting could upset my electrolytes enough to make me pass out?"

"Yeah. I was just thinking that with you being… you know, *pregnant*, I shouldn't take any chances."

"You were being a good friend," I say with a tight smile. "I just wish that they would release me."

Olive's phone buzzes, and she checks it. She glances at me nervously.

"Okay, who has been texting you?" I ask, exasperated.

"Uhhh…. don't get mad…" she says.

"At what, exactly?" I narrow my eyes at her.

"I might have called Jett?" she says, making a don't-kill-me face.

"You WHAT?" I say, stunned.

"Well, you are his girlfriend," she says. "And you are carrying his baby…"

Tears prick my eyes. "I don't want to see him."

"No no, we'd just finished talking about how you were going to talk to him—"

"I don't want him to come running because he feels bad!" I say, my face crumpling.

Her phone buzzes again. "I'm sure that's not why he's coming."

"Wait, he's coming here?! Now??" I howl, tears streaming down my face. "No! No way!"

She looks at me for a second, then gets frank with me. "Look, I know you don't like people seeing you cry. I get that. But you're about to tell this guy you love him. Do you think that maybe you can take your foot off the gas a little, just for him?"

I sniffle. "I— I don't know…"

"Well, he's here. I'm about to go get him, okay?" She moves toward the curtain-covered door.

"Wait!" When she glances back, I beseech her. "Just Jett, okay?"

Olive smiles. "I promise."

She pulls open the curtains and vanishes. I'm left on the hospital bed, itchy and uncomfortable and pretty much just wishing I was anywhere else. Jett pokes his head in a minute later, dressed in workout clothes.

His brow is furrowed. "Hey."

"Hi," I say, squirming in the bed. I'm acutely aware that I'm only wearing a hospital gown on my top half. I cross my one good arm over my chest.

"Can I come in?" he says.

I nod. He pushes the curtains aside, and then closes them after himself.

"You're okay?" he says. I nod, unsure how to even begin to tell him how I feel.

I look at him for a second, all six feet and three inches of bearded, tattooed bad boy. He's looking at me with a concerned expression, dark brows hunched over dark blue eyes.

I'm conscious of every breath I draw. For a second, we just look at each other, taking one another's measure. I start to open my mouth, but he just shakes his head.

"No. No talking," he says, striding over to the bed. He leans down and brushes some of my hair out of my face. It feels so natural and so right that I lean against his hand for a second.

Then he kisses me, placing every single ounce of emotion that he has in the meeting of our lips, our tongues dancing together. He tastes a little salty; I think he just came from working out. I reach my free hand up to cup the back of his neck and bring him closer, and he buries his fingers in my hair.

I didn't even realize how much I need this, need his kiss, his scent, until he touches me. A needy sound comes out of the back of my throat, and I can feel tears welling up. I feel utterly vulnerable to him, like my heart is exposed for all to see.

But at the same time, I know in my heart that he will wrap me in his arms and protect me. That feeling of my heart squeezing, every time I look into his eyes?

I know what that is. I just have to have the courage to say it.

When we finally pause for breath, he leans his forehead against mine.

"I'm so sorry," he whispers. "You have to know that I… I love you, Cady."

My tears overflow. "I love you too, Jett. I figured that out a while ago, but I felt like…"

"Like you didn't want to say anything, because you were risking everything?"

"Yes," I say, nodding my head. My voice is thick with emotion. "I'm sorry."

"Whatever happens, I want you to know that I do want you in my life. And the baby too. I want to take care of you both."

I don't know how to respond to that, so I just reach up for another kiss. I move over a little, and he sits down a bit awkwardly on the edge of the hospital bed.

Slowly, Jett pulls away from the kiss, running his thumb along my jawline. "I want to rip up the contract terminating my parental rights."

"Oh! I mean… I guess that isn't really needed anymore, is it?"

"No. Not only is it not needed, it's not wanted. I want to make sure that my intentions are crystal clear this time."

I purse my lips. "And what are your intentions, exactly?"

He grins. "Why, I plan to make you mine, in every sense of the word. Marriage, a house together… I've already done a good job of knocking you up…"

His smile is infectious. I grin.

"We can talk about those things, in time."

"I'm ripping up that contract as soon as I get my hands on it," he says. "That's that."

I make a little hmm sound, but I'm pleased. He looks around the room, his grin fading.

"Why did you come here? It isn't anything serious, is it?"

My cheeks flush.

"It's not a big deal. I had a little... morning sickness," I say, hesitant to have it spoken aloud. The phrase feels weird coming out of my mouth. "And I guess my electrolytes got imbalanced. I'm not even sure why I'm here. Olive just freaked out a bit. Now I'm under observation, I guess because I fainted."

"And everything is okay with..." he swallows. Maybe he's having the same issue as I am. "With the baby?"

"Totally. I actually just had my first official test," I say.

He looks surprised. "Did they do... what is it called? Where they run a magnetic wand over your stomach and get a picture?"

"An ultrasound?" I say, trying not to laugh. "No, definitely not. It's way too early for that. They just did a pregnancy test."

Jett exhales. "Okay. Well, what about Seattle? Are you still thinking about moving?"

I shake my head. "It would be accepting a huge promotion, starting their new office out there. And Olive was asked to move to Seattle too... I think I would be crazy not to do it for a couple of years. But... I think a lot of that depends on you and your career."

His brow hunches. "Yeah. I'm not sure what I'll do, but we can work something out. Just as long as you and... the baby are safe."

He pales a little when he says the baby. I bite my lip.

"It's okay to be completely freaked out," I tell him. "Having a baby is like... a pretty fucking big deal."

Jett looks a little sheepish. "It doesn't seem real yet."

"No, it definitely doesn't. But it'll be here before we know it. And we have a ton of stuff to sort out before then."

"Like almost everything," he muses.

"But that could be a good thing!" I say.

"We'll just say that it is," he says with a wink. He accidentally bumps my IVs, reminding me of where we are.

"Alright, enough of this," I say. "I'm going to call a nurse to unhook me from these things."

"Whoa, there," he says. "Is it going to kill you to sit here and let everyone fuss over you for the next couple of hours?"

I wrinkle my nose. "Maybe."

"Nope. You are staying put. That's an order," he says. He picks up my hand and places a kiss on the back of it, then stands up. "You're carrying my baby, so you stay as long as they think you need to stay."

I want to protest, but his declaration makes my heart swell with emotion.

"Okay," I sigh. "Just so you know, I do not find this charming."

He grins. "You say that, but I think you do. You love me, remember?"

I bite my lip. "I really do."

"Then trust me to take care of you."

"I do! Or... I will," I say, shifting in the bed.

He peeks outside the curtain, then comes back and sits on the bed once more. He looks down into my eyes, and takes my hand.

"It's going to be fine, Cady. I promise. I think the three of us will do really well."

"Yeah?" I ask.

"Yeah," he says. "You'll see."

Emotion blooms from deep in my chest. I lean forward and kiss him, thinking of how lucky I am.

"Yes, we will."

EPILOGUE

*C*ady - Six Months Later

I stretch in my chair at the new office, arching my back. My baby bump sticks out even further, pushing against my desk and levering me away in my office chair. I eye my ever-expending stomach; I'm wearing the stretchy black maternity skirt that I favor and a white tank top, plus a pink cardigan. I pick a couple of Milo's hairs off my skirt, then make a face.

"Oooh," I say, wincing. "Careful with my organs in there, kid."

The fun new thing that my little boy is doing is doing what feels like kick flips inside my belly. Putting my hand on my stomach to try to calm the baby, I rise from my chair to walk a little. I look out my wall to ceiling glass windows at the downtown skyline of Seattle.

It's still unbelievable to me that I'm here. The first couple months of my pregnancy were hard as hell on my body… and that's not even considering the whole moving across the country thing.

Luckily, Jett is here with me, and Olive too. It took Jett and I a bit to figure out how we were going to do it: Jett had his job and his house, I had my house and my baby to worry about.

But Jett managed to keep most of his clients through telecommuting and once per month trips. And both of us sold our homes, finding a perfect three-bedroom home on the outskirts of Seattle.

As for my health, I've been super pro-active during my pregnancy. Yoga, running, birthing classes… Seattle is the place to be for expectant mothers, it seems.

The baby won't stop kicking. I fold my hands over my belly and pace. It usually calms him down.

Today is a challenge of sorts. It seems like everything that could go wrong has gone wrong. First, one of my clients was a no show during our depositions, apparently having overslept. Then I wasn't paying attention, barreling down the hall and talking on my phone. I ran right into one of the first year associates, who was carrying a cup of hot coffee.

Unsurprisingly, the hot coffee ended up all over the right side of my skirt. That was at least an hour ago, but it's only just now drying. Damn Seattle humidity.

To top it all off, I got the yearly photos back that the firm forces everyone to take. After looking at the proofs, I locked myself in my office and bawled at how fat I've become.

So yeah, today has been a test. Of what, I do not know. I just know that hormones and emotions are running high.

At least my pacing has calmed the baby down a little. I bounce for another minute, then head back to my desk.

As I'm settling in, Olive knocks on my open door. She

looks gorgeous as ever, wearing a perfect black silk dress with a huge black bow on one shoulder. "Hey, you."

"Hey," I say, trying not to be envious of her ability to wear normal clothes.

She looks at me, her gaze narrowing. "You look tired. Are you feeling alright?"

"Yup," I nod. "Except there is this creature feeding off of my essence. Everything else is alright."

"Ha ha," she says. "Where are your shoes?"

I turn and look at my black flats. I wore heels until month five, and then it was laughable to think about continuing. "Oh, under the desk. I'll put them back on if anyone I don't know comes by."

"Well, you might want to put them on. I'm taking you to lunch." She smiles, a little too broadly.

I cast a suspicious gaze in her direction. "Why?"

"Can't a girl just want to take her best friend to lunch? Besides, I got reservations at Altura. You loved that place, according to Jett."

I brighten up. "I did! They do the best cannoli. Just thinking about it makes my mouth water."

Olive beams. "Great! Get your shoes and make sure you bundle up. It's cold outside. I'll meet you in the lobby downstairs, alright?"

I nod. She shuttles out of my office, leaving me to get my big blue wool maternity coat on. I put on my coat and my shoes, groaning a bit when my sore feet hit the soles. It's almost time to go up a size in shoes, if I continue to hold so much water.

A few minutes later, I head down to the elevator. When I hit the lobby, Olive is waiting.

"Did you hear that the lead witness in my case might have bailed?" she says. We both shield our eyes as we head out into the bright light of downtown, here amongst the tall, grey buildings. "Oh, I think that's our Uber right there."

I'm so glad to have Olive with me, because even though Altura is technically walkable from here, no way do I want to try. Luckily, she didn't even consult me, she just called for an Uber without me. We walk down to the curb, where our car is waiting. I shiver against the cold breeze that rattles through downtown.

"No, I didn't hear anything. What happened?" I say as I ease into the new Toyota. We pull out and take a right.

"So the guy, Tony Grimes, is now worried that his family might be in danger if he testifies in open court." She wrinkles her nose. "He knew that from the get go, but now he's *concerned*, whatever that means."

"Do you think he's going to testify?" I ask.

"I don't know. We'll sit down with him tomorrow and see if we can allay his concerns." She pushes a hand through her long red hair. "It's kind of a tense situation."

We chat for a few minutes, and then the car pulls up outside Altura. It's a simple little glass doorfront, without any showy stuff. It's pretty unassuming. That's one of the things that I think makes it special.

"Here we are," Olive announces.

We both get out of the car, walking up to the restaurant. I squint.

"Are you sure they're open?" I ask her. "It looks… empty. It's never empty."

"I'm sure," she says with a wink. She looks secretive as she opens the door for me. "You first."

I glare at Olive. She knows something, and she's not telling. I try to think of what it could be. My birthday was two months ago, and we're past the New Year already. Could it be a really early baby shower?

I don't actually think I know when a baby shower is even supposed to happen, I think. *That must be it.*

I head inside the restaurant, which is almost empty, the tables all set and the bar polished. There is only one waiter, standing there ready to take our coats. I pull my coat off and hand it over to him.

"Hi," I smile at him, a little puzzled.

"Miss Ellis," he says, bowing. "We have a table for you, right this way."

I turn to Olive, but she hasn't even taken her coat off.

"Aren't you coming?" I ask, my brow furrowing.

"In a little while," she says, waving off any concern. "Don't worry, you're where you're meant to be."

"What?" I say, but she backs toward the door.

"If you would, please?" the waiter says.

"Ummm… all right…" I say, shaking my head. I follow him into another room, which is cleared out except for one white linen-covered table and two chairs.

Jett is there, handsome in an immaculate dark grey suit. Even now, his dark hair and tattoos give me chills, even though I am irritable. He grins when he spots me, standing up.

"Jett!" I scold him. "What the hell is going on?"

"Cady," he says, pulling out a chair for me. "Sit."

I waddle over to the chair and sit down, internally sighing. He rubs my shoulders for a few seconds, which is heavenly.

"This is a baby shower?" I murmur, letting my eyes close a little.

He chuckles. "No."

I open my my eyes as he releases me, taking his seat beside me. "Then why are we here?"

"You aren't going to make this easy for me, are you?" he jokes.

"Make what easy? Baby, you know that I don't like surprises…" I say, rubbing my baby bump. "Also, your son doesn't like them either. He won't sit still."

He holds up his hand. "Okay, okay. I was going to ask the kitchen for dinner first, but I think you'll be more comfortable if I just say it."

"Say what—" I begin, but I cut myself off when he reaches in his pocket and produces a black velvet ring box. I look at him, my hands flying to my mouth. "Is that—"

"Shhh," Jett says, trying not to laugh. "Just let me do this the right way."

Tears start leaking down both sides of my face as he moves from his chair, kneeling before me. My heart feels like it's beating so fast that it might break free of my chest. When he opens the ring box with a snap, I'm overwhelmed.

He's chosen a beautiful emerald, flanked on both sides by diamonds. He clears his throat, and I look at him, trying not to cry too loudly.

"Cady Anne Ellison," he says, his voice tense. "From the day I met you, I knew that you were special. I love your passion, and your intelligence blows me away. I even like your cat, even though I'm not a cat person. I love you, Cady."

I am trying to hold back my sobs. I manage, "I love you too."

He gives me that million dollar smile. "Will you do me the honor of being my wife?"

I nod emphatically, too choked up to speak. He plucks the ring out of the box, and holds his hand out for mine. I shakingly put my small hand in his big one, and he slips the ring on.

Then he stands and helps me to my feet, dipping me

just a little as he kisses me. I curl my hands around his nape as I kiss him back, sucking in lungfuls of his clean scent.

In that moment, I know without a shadow of a doubt that I am going to be happy and cared for the rest of my life.

GET A FREE BOOK!

Join my mailing list to be the first to know of new releases, free books, special prices and other author giveaways.

http://freehotcontemporary.com

ALSO BY JESSA JAMES

Bad Boy Billionaires

A Virgin for the Billionaire

Her Rockstar Billionaire

Her Secret Billionaire

A Bargain with the Billionaire

Billionaire Box Set 1-4

The Virgin Pact

The Teacher and the Virgin

His Virgin Nanny

His Dirty Virgin

Club V

Unravel

Undone

Uncover

Cowboy Romance

How To Love A Cowboy

How To Hold A Cowboy

Beg Me

Valentine Ever After

Covet/Crave

Kiss Me Again

Handy

Bad Behavior

Bad Reputation

Dr. Hottie

Hot as Hell

Pretend I'm Yours

Rock Star

Capture

Control

ABOUT THE AUTHOR

Jessa James grew up on the East Coast but always suffered a severe case of wanderlust. She's lived in six states, had a variety of jobs and always comes back to her first true love – writing. Jessa works full time as a writer, eats too much dark chocolate, has an iced-coffee and Cheetos addiction, and can't get enough of sexy alpha males who know exactly what they want – and aren't afraid to say it. Dominant, alpha-male insta-luv is her favorite to read (and write).

Sign up HERE for Jessa's Newsletter:

http://jessajamesauthor.com/mailing-list/

Follow me on BookBub:

www.ingramcontent.com/pod-product-compliance
Lightning Source LLC
LaVergne TN
LVHW011818060526
838200LV00053B/3822